# She Hadn't Seen That Look For A While, But She Recognized It Just The Same.

It was a pure, ornery, dance-with-the-devil dare.

Something about the way he watched her, his blue eyes full of mischief, his crooked smile teasing, took her to a place and time where everything had once been special and right between them. And she forgot, for the moment, that she had kept guard of her feelings around him. Forgot, even, why she'd thought there was still some reason to keep her distance.

Dear Reader,

Twenty years ago in May, the first Silhouette romance was published, and in 2000 we're celebrating our 20th anniversary all year long! Celebrate with us—and start with six powerful, passionate, provocative love stories from Silhouette Desire.

Elizabeth Bevarly offers a MAN OF THE MONTH so tempting that we decided to call it *Dr. Irresistible!* Enjoy this sexy tale about a single-mom nurse who enlists a handsome doctor to pose as her husband at her tenth high school reunion. The wonderful miniseries LONE STAR FAMILIES: THE LOGANS, by bestselling author Leanne Banks, continues with *Expecting His Child,* a sensual romance about a woman carrying the child of her family's nemesis after a stolen night of passion.

Ever-talented Cindy Gerard returns to Desire with *In His Loving Arms,* in which a pregnant widow is reunited with the man who's haunted her dreams for seven years. Sheikhs abound in Alexandra Sellers' *Sheikh's Honor,* a new addition to her dramatic miniseries SONS OF THE DESERT. The Desire theme promotion, THE BABY BANK, about women who find love unexpectedly when seeking sperm donors, continues with Metsy Hingle's *The Baby Bonus.* And newcomer Kathie DeNosky makes her Desire debut with *Did You Say Married?!,* in which the heroine wakes up in Vegas next to a sexy cowboy who turns out to be her newly wed husband.

What a lineup! So this May, for Mother's Day, why not treat your mom—and yourself—to all six of these highly sensual and emotional love stories from Silhouette Desire!

Enjoy!

*Joan Marlow Golan*

Joan Marlow Golan
Senior Editor, Silhouette Desire

Please address questions and book requests to:
Silhouette Reader Service
U.S.: 3010 Walden Ave., P.O. Box 1325, Buffalo, NY 14269
Canadian: P.O. Box 609, Fort Erie, Ont. L2A 5X3

# In His Loving Arms
## CINDY GERARD

Silhouette®

Desire.

Published by Silhouette Books
America's Publisher of Contemporary Romance

This book is dedicated to my editor, Karen Kosztolnyik.

Karen, for your generous enthusiasm, your light touch
and for those cute little hearts you draw in the margins
of my manuscripts, which always make me smile,
I thank you. I'm glad you were with me for this special
landmark, my 10th Desire book.

 SILHOUETTE BOOKS

ISBN 0-373-76293-3

IN HIS LOVING ARMS

Visit Silhouette at www.eHarlequin.com

**Printed in U.S.A.**

**Books by Cindy Gerard**

Silhouette Desire

*The Cowboy Takes a Lady* #957
*Lucas: The Loner* #975
*\*The Bride Wore Blue* #1012
*\*A Bride for Abel Greene* #1052
*\*A Bride for Crimson Falls* #1076
*†The Outlaw's Wife* #1175
*†Marriage, Outlaw Style* #1185
*†The Outlaw Jesse James* #1198
*Lone Star Prince* #1256
*In His Loving Arms* #1293

*Northern Lights Brides
†Outlaw Hearts

---

## CINDY GERARD

celebrates her tenth book for Silhouette with the publication of *In His Loving Arms*. If asked "What's your idea of heaven?" Cindy Gerard would say a warm sun, a cool breeze, pan pizza and a good book. If she had to settle for one of the four, she'd opt for the book, with the pizza running a close second. Inspired by the pleasure she's received from the books she's read and her longtime love affair with her husband, Tom, Cindy now creates her own warm, evocative stories about compelling characters and complex relationships.

All that reading must have paid off, because since winning the Waldenbooks Award for Best Selling Series Romance for a First-Time Author, Cindy has gone on to win the prestigious Colorado Romance Writers' Award of Excellence, *Romantic Times Magazine* W.I.S.H. Awards, Career Achievement and Reviewers' Choice nominations, and the Romance Writers of America's RITA nomination for Best Short Contemporary Romance.

# IT'S OUR 20<sup>th</sup> ANNIVERSARY!
## We'll be celebrating all year,
## Continuing with these fabulous titles,
## On sale in May 2000.

### Romance

 **#1444 Mercenary's Woman**
Diana Palmer

**#1445 Too Hard To Handle**
Rita Rainville

 **#1446 A Royal Mission**
Elizabeth August

**#1447 Tall, Strong & Cool Under Fire**
Marie Ferrarella

**#1448 Hannah Gets a Husband**
Julianna Morris

**#1449 Her Sister's Child**
Lilian Darcy

### Desire

 **#1291 Dr. Irresistible**
Elizabeth Bevarly

 **#1292 Expecting His Child**
Leanne Banks

**#1293 In His Loving Arms**
Cindy Gerard

 **#1294 Sheikh's Honor**
Alexandra Sellers

 **#1295 The Baby Bonus**
Metsy Hingle

**#1296 Did You Say Married?!**
Kathie DeNosky

### Intimate Moments

 **#1003 Rogue's Reform**
Marilyn Pappano

**#1004 The Cowboy's Hidden Agenda**
Kathleen Creighton

**#1005 In a Heartbeat**
Carla Cassidy

 **#1006 Anything for Her Marriage**
Karen Templeton

**#1007 Every Little Thing**
Linda Winstead Jones

 **#1008 Remember the Night**
Linda Castillo

### Special Edition

 **#1321 The Kincaid Bride**
Jackie Merritt

**#1322 The Millionaire She Married**
Christine Rimmer

**#1323 Warrior's Embrace**
Peggy Webb

**#1324 The Sheik's Arranged Marriage**
Susan Mallery

**#1325 Sullivan's Child**
Gail Link

**#1326 Wild Mustang**
Jane Toombs

# One

He was my brother in every way but blood. Now he's gone and it's too late to do anything but miss him.
—Excerpt from Mark Remington's journal

At the top of the hill was his brother's house. Inside the house was his brother's widow. Outside, wishing he was anywhere but where he was, Mark Remington sat in his car alone in the dark.

Parked at the curb, hardly aware of the steady purr of his Viper's idling motor, Mark heard Grace McKenzie's concern about her daughter play through his mind like a bad dream. *Something's wrong, Mark. I know she's still grieving, I know she needs time, but she won't open up to us. She won't let us help…. She won't tell us what's happening with her. Please go check on her. You two used to be so close. Maybe she'll talk to you.*

He thought about what Grace had said—and about how much he didn't want to be here. But what he wanted didn't change a damn thing. It didn't change the fact that except for the funeral three months ago, he'd avoided Lauren for seven years. It didn't change the fact that he couldn't turn around and run. Not until he saw her. Not until he made sure she was all right—then he'd get out of her life. Again.

He tightened his grip on the steering wheel when a woman's silhouette ghosted slowly past a shaded window. Dead-of-night black, as bleak as the prospect of confronting her, closed in around him like a shroud. Dragging his gaze away, he sank deeper into the rich leather of the bucket seat as the tension knotting his shoulders and souring in his gut intensified to an acid burn.

It had been past midnight in the Sierras when he'd snagged the Viper's keys, roared out of Sunrise Ranch and headed up the coast to Frisco. He glanced at the digital clock on the dash. Glowing green numbers blinked 2:55 a.m. He swiped a hand over his jaw. Insane. It had been insane to take off in the middle of the night, but impulse always ruled over sanity. It least, it did with him. He'd wanted to get this over with—even more than he'd wanted to ignore Lauren's mother's call.

After the first awkward "hello" and "it's been a long time," Grace McKenzie had gotten down to business. The business of shaming him into coming to see Lauren.

He stared into the thickness of the July night. Grace was wrong about one thing. The last person in the world Lauren would want to talk to was him. Just like this was the last place on earth he wanted to be.

His grip on the gearshift flexed and relaxed as he wrestled one final urge to whip the car into gear and take the easy way out. After all, that's what he did best, right? Cut and run. Save his pride.

Pride aside, even reason told him to get the hell away from her—but then reason had little to do with getting him here.

A tight fist of pain curled around his chest. They'd buried his brother three months ago, in April. Nate was gone and Mark was only here now because Lauren was in trouble. And because—as Grace had reminded him—he was family. As family, he was duty-bound.

He let go of a cynical snort. Honest truth? His sense of duty hadn't played much of a part in getting him this far. Good stout whiskey had. He'd needed a little midnight courage. Stone-cold sober, he'd never be ready for this encounter. Stone-cold sober, he wouldn't be sitting here—thinking about

Nate, thinking about Lauren and about all the times in his life he'd answered the call to run.

He shrugged off the urge that had never worked its way out of his system and finally cut the motor. Dragging his palms roughly across a day's growth of beard, he drew a fortifying breath, then shouldered open the door. He'd offered Lauren a shoulder to cry on often enough in the past. He could be a man. He could manage one more time.

"Real hero material, that's me," he muttered with grim sarcasm. *As generous in deed as he was fearless behind the wheel.* Wasn't that the line some sensation-seeking staff writer for *Nascar Racing News* had tagged on him once?

Once, a long time ago.

Just like it had been a long time since he'd seen the checkered flag and the winner's circle. A long time. A lot of long nights.

He stared, again, at the house. Dammit, he didn't want to be here.

"Well, ace," he muttered darkly. "It doesn't matter what you want."

What mattered—what had always mattered—was Lauren.

Shoving his hands deep into the back pockets of his jeans, he headed up the walk.

# Two

I don't know what I expected, but it wasn't to find her so broken, or that the wanting would still be so strong.
—Excerpt from Mark Remington's journal

The doorbell chimed a second time. Lauren's gaze swung to the mantel clock—3:00 a.m. Guilt cut deep, drew blood. Her parents cared, bless them, but why couldn't they just leave her alone?

She'd expected them to show up. But not in the middle of the night—and not this soon, even though the lecture her mother had delivered long distance from L.A. yesterday had been more severe than usual. As it always was these days when she called, it had also been overloaded with concern.

*Honey, you can't keep shutting yourself off from your family and your friends this way. Let us help you through this.*

*I'm fine, Mom. I just need some time.*

*I know it's hard, sweetheart. But it's hard for us not being there for you. It's been three months since…since the funeral, honey. Two since we've seen you.*

*I know…I know how long it's been.*

Lauren didn't take any pride in her ability to recite their conversation word for word. Just like she didn't hold out any hope that her stock replies offered her parents any assurance. For their sake, she was sorry, but she'd fallen into a hole—a deep, dark hole after Nate's death—and she couldn't muster the strength to set their minds at ease or to claw her way out.

The doorbell chimed again. She forked her fingers through her hair, held the heavy blond mass back from her face as if the action could forestall what now appeared inevitable. She hadn't wanted them to see her like this. She'd lost weight. Her long hair was as limp and listless as her coffee-colored eyes.

She was tired.

It was more than feeding the hungry bite of pain that exhausted her. It was more than despondency that immobilized her and kept her from figuring

out a way to deal with a whole new set of problems. It was more even, than guilt, for forcing her
parents out at this ungodly hour, that weighed like
lead.

It was so much more.

Tears stung. She blinked them back. Now was
not the time, this was not the way she had wanted
to tell them.

She looked toward the door and, resigned, rose
from the corner of the sofa. Fatigue hit like a club,
dizzying her. She battled back the familiar weakness then cinched the belt of her chenille robe
tighter around her waist. Walking stiffly to the
foyer, she drew back her shoulders and swung
open the door.

"Hello, Lauren."

Her knees threatened to buckle when she saw
Mark, not her parents, standing there. She gripped
the door to keep from swaying, but nothing could
help brace against the barrage of emotions that
blindsided her.

The hot pulse of shock hummed through her
blood, stole her breath—and for the first time in
months, an emotion other than grief or despair
crashed through the barriers she'd erected. Memories swamped her, mingled with the moment and
the reminders of feelings that had once been fresh
and young and new.

But it wasn't a memory that faced her now. It
was Mark—a Mark she didn't know anymore.

Everything about him registered at once. The midnight-blue eyes that stared back at her were edged with fatigue, the square jaw stubbled and insolent. Hair the color of sun-dusted wheat fell belligerently across his brow and bore the mark of several harsh rakings by the long fingers that were tucked with staged casualness into the back pockets of his faded black jeans.

He smelled of a dark, musky cologne—a familiar scent, one she'd always associated with him and had never been able to forget. And he smelled of the whiskey he had evidently spent half the night drinking and had never been a part of the Mark she used to know.

The regrets, for who he was and the road he'd chosen, for her own unexpected physical reaction to his stunning, if jaded beauty, made her defensive and edgy and achingly aware that although her husband was dead, she was still very much alive.

The rush of it scared her. The shock and the shame of it forced her to attack.

"What are you doing here?"

He met the distrust in her eyes without flinching. Then for too long he just looked at her. For too long she let him, until the dark detachment in his eyes changed to pity.

"You look like hell, Lauren."

His voice was a velvet purr, gravelly and low, hinting at excesses she'd read about, hadn't wanted to believe. Yet affection outdistanced the censure in his words and stirred more memories—gentle ones—that she hadn't been prepared for and knew only one way to defend.

Anger boiled up, instant and hot, frighteningly self-righteous. "And you can go to hell."

Ashamed of her unprovoked attack, yet afraid of all the feelings crashing in on her, she slammed the door in his face.

He was way ahead of her. He flattened his palm on the heavy wooden door. With little effort, he wedged his shoulder through the narrow opening and shoved into her foyer.

His eyes were cold, blank of emotion. "Consensus is, I'll do just that someday...but it looks like this is as close as I'll get tonight."

Without another word, he shrugged out of his jacket. The supple, expensive leather looked old and comfortable. Like everything about her reaction to him, it was disconcerting to realize she recognized it. If he hadn't been wearing his racing gear in the thousands of photos taken of him during his career, he'd been wearing that jacket. Even the producers of a series of glitzy commercials and billboards promoting everything from the Nascar circuit to expensive cologne to designer jeans had recognized the appeal of Mark Remington in black leather and a bedroom smile. The jacket had been tailor-made and carefully fit to perpetuate the "look," the rebel image his racing fans still adored even two years after he'd inexplicably walked away from a career that could have rivaled the Earnharts and the Andrettis if he'd stuck with it.

But then he never stuck with anything, Lauren reminded herself. He never stayed. He ran. Always—like he'd run seven years ago.

She returned his stare icily, surprised when he looked away, notching his chin the way the boy she had loved used as a defense. She refused to remember that boy—the one whose sadness had drawn her from the first day he'd come to live with the people next door.

That boy was gone. The man was here now. And whether she liked the man or not, it was the man who held her reluctant attention.

The wear and tear of a reckless lifestyle that made good press, even beyond the racing scene, would have ravaged any other man's physical appeal. But he wasn't any other man. He was Mark Remington, America's ultimate male, the bad boy who had gotten by with it because he wasn't quite as bad as the worst and because he had a face and body that could accelerate the heart rates of women aged sixteen to sixty.

His escapades were legend—on and off the track. His slow, sexy grin had been pure gold to both the racing world and his bankroll. His hard-living, hard-loving reputation had been money-making grist for the gossip mills. The public had adored him…because of his beauty, because of his fearlessness, because of his good-natured contempt for anything that had vaguely resembled a principle. He'd flaunted that contempt with the same disregard he'd displayed toward his trophies. And his women. Then he'd just dropped out of sight.

Yes, the public loved him…and Lauren wanted very much to hate him. Her memory flashed to a night she'd tried to block for seven years. Even knowing that what had happened between them was more her fault than his, she still wanted to hate him—for the strain it had brought to her marriage and for the pain it had brought to a man who had never understood what mountain had cast the shadow that had always loomed between them.

And she wanted to hate him because she knew what no one else did—that he'd left to get away from her. He'd run. He'd run, like he always ran and denied her the chance to sort it all out, to tell him…to tell him that all was forgiven, all was forgotten. To put it all in perspective.

It was an old want and long nurtured. And while it consumed more energy than she had to commit, it would have taken more to conceal it.

With a weary shake of his head and a roll of a broad shoulder, he read her contempt for exactly what it was and braced against the ice in her eyes. "Got anything to drink?"

It was so in character, she almost laughed. "I doubt there's anything strong enough."

He smiled tightly, made a quick assessment of his surroundings and ambled to the dry bar in the corner of the living room. "Guess I'll just have to chance it."

He looked totally out of place in the old Victorian home that she and Nate had lovingly furnished with period pieces and sentimental collections. The house was warm and subtly elegant. Mark was anything but. He was cool and jaded, dangerously edgy as he inspected the limited bar selection.

"Join me?" He raised a snifter of brandy and a golden brow. His whiskey-roughened voice coaxed like a caress when she gave a crisp shake of her head. "Oh, come on, Lauren. Live dangerously— besides, you look like you could use it."

She wrapped her robe tighter around her waist and settled stiffly onto the corner of the sofa. "Whatever you came here to say, just say it."

He took his time rounding the bar, then leaned back against it. Propping his elbows behind him, he studied her, then the amber liquid in the snifter. "I guess the best thing about wallowing in self-pity is that you don't have to deal with anyone's grief but your own."

While his tone was gentle, his words sliced to the bone. The accusation was so unexpected and so cutting, she caught her breath—then fought a crushing onslaught of shame.

She hadn't yet recovered when he lifted his gaze from the brandy.

"Has it occurred to you, Lauren, that you aren't the only one who loved him?"

She'd been prepared for sarcasm, for an insult, but not for the raw pain that edged his words—or for a vulnerability she'd never suspected was hidden under all that brass. She felt herself softening toward him before remembering who he was. Once, maybe, he'd been vulnerable. Once a long time ago. And while she resented him for what he'd become, she hated herself more for the weakness she'd shown one night in his arms.

"What has occurred to me," she said, working to keep her voice steady, "is that there are far too many wrongs in this life and far too few rights."

Eyes so blue, and so unlike Nate's soft green, clouded with pain before wrenching away from hers and back to the swirl of brandy. "Roughly translated, too bad it wasn't me who died instead of Nate."

Silence settled, wretched and raw—a silence she should have filled with denial.

That's not what she'd meant. But she couldn't get the words out to tell him he was wrong. She could never wish him dead. They'd been friends once. She'd loved him once—but she couldn't distance herself from her own grief long enough to lessen his.

Cold as stone, she could only watch as he tossed back the last of his drink, knowing her silence fed into his thoughts—thoughts she could read as if he'd spoken aloud. *I was the one who always lived on the edge. The one who repeatedly flirted with death. Nate had never even had a speeding ticket. Yet it was Nate who was in the wrong place at the wrong time and died at the hands of a drunk driver.*

Drifting deeper into guilt, she lowered her head. They'd both lost Nate. A wave of emotion swamped her—so big and so full of love and loss and need that it terrified her.

Mark terrified her more—because of the feelings he'd unearthed that she'd buried with Nate. Because of the things he made her remember.

Because of the things he made her forget.

Nate. Oh, God. For the first time in three months, her every thought hadn't centered around Nate. And she wasn't ready to let him go. Neither was she capable of being kind—not when she hurt this badly.

She drew a bracing breath, got a slippery grip on her composure and refused to think about what kind of a monster that made her. Ignoring the bleakness in Mark's eyes, she told herself she didn't dare let him know what seeing him again had done to her. Just like she couldn't tell him that Nate had left her with a problem so massive she was lost for a solution.

She watched him walk to the window and stare into the predawn darkness. The ticking of the clock marked the time and the tension before he finally spoke again.

"Your mother called."

She squared her shoulders, stared at her tightly clasped hands, finally understanding why he was here. "I'm sorry she bothered you."

He rolled a shoulder. "She's worried about you."

"And sent *you* to straighten me out?" She actually heard herself laugh as he turned to face her. The brittle, humorless sound jarred the silence like the aftershock of a California quake. "Isn't that a little like sending the fox to watch the henhouse?"

His smile was shallow and careful and never went further than his mouth. "Your mother is a remarkably wonderful, remarkably naive woman who has evidently never read a gossip column or a tabloid. Somehow, she's managed to put me on freeze frame somewhere in the vicinity of my twelfth birthday."

A memory, a good one, broke through, warmed her. Because it was the first thing that had felt good in a very long time, she allowed herself a moment to hold it close. "The year you rescued her tabby from the tree in the front yard."

"A regular Boy Scout, that's me." He raised his glass in mock salute and knocked back another swallow.

Wiping his mouth with the back of the hand that

held the empty glass, he faced her squarely. "So, what's the story, Lauren? She says you're not eating...I believe it. Obviously, you're not sleeping. You look like a damn ghost."

Anger rose from the ashes of sentiment. "For the life of me, I don't understand how you charm so many women into your bed." Or how he could make her shift, in a heartbeat, from soft sentiment to mercurial anger, when, for the past three months, if she hadn't felt pain or panic, she'd felt nothing.

His blue eyes bored into hers. "We're not talking about my bed or my women...we're talking about you. Lauren...." He crossed the room and sank down on the sofa facing her. "What in God's name are you trying to do to yourself?"

She stared hard at her hands, vaguely aware that her fingers, wrapped tightly around each other, had turned white. What was she trying to do? She was trying to survive. She was trying to distance herself from anything and everything that made her feel—because when she felt, the pain was unbearable.

So she did the only thing she could. She closed off, she closed up. "What I do with my life is not your concern."

She didn't have to look at him to feel the heat of his gaze pressing for explanations, willing her to fill in the blanks, tempting her to lean on him when that was the last thing she could let herself do. Just like he was the last person on earth she could count on.

She couldn't tell anyone about the mess Nate had left her in. She especially couldn't tell Mark.

She flinched when he reached out, touched her. He swore under his breath, firmed his mouth, then cupped her shoulders in a gentle grip and turned her to face him.

"Nate's gone, Lauren."

How could his voice be so tender when his words were so harshly true? She tried to pull away. He held her fast. Forced her to listen.

"If I could bring him back I'd do it. If going after that drunken scum who ran him off the road would bring him back, I'd do it. But I can't. And neither can you."

Like the nightmares that haunted her, memories closed in on her like a coffin—the late-night visit from the police, the moment when denial knuckled under to blinding, excruciating grief. They crowded, cloyed, clogging her breath, knotting in her chest like a grisly fist.

Desperate to block them, she wrenched away from Mark's hands, away from a touch she should hate but suddenly needed more than she needed to breathe.

She rose shakily to her feet, walked on unsteady legs to the bar—and got blindsided by the recurrent

nausea that had badgered her since the funeral. It
slammed into her without warning.

She closed her eyes, then swayed against the
bar. From a distance, she heard Mark call her
name. Through a haze of slipping sensations, she
watched him rise from the sofa. She saw, rather
than heard his mouth form a violent curse as he
lunged across the room. Sensed more than felt the
strength of his arms enfold her as everything
around her went cobwebby and black.

Unconsciousness was the easy way out. She
wanted it. She craved it, drifted toward it willingly,
on some unguarded level aware of Mark's heat, the
soothing, musky scent of his cologne…and the
memories that wouldn't leave her alone.

"Easy, Lauren. I've got you."

Damning the rising nausea that clawed again and
dragged her back toward lucidity, she fought his
hands, shoved weakly against him. "Let me go."

"Not until you're steady."

"Mark, please. Let…let me go. I…I'm going to
be sick."

He stalled, no longer than an instant, then swept
her into his arms and headed off in search of a
bathroom.

They made it just in time for her to drop to her
knees and retch violently into the stool. Too sick
to be embarrassed, too grateful for his gentle
hands, she let him hold her hair away from her

face, rub her back, murmur words of comfort as she emptied the meager contents of her stomach.

When it was over, she couldn't muster the strength or the pride to ask him to leave. She collapsed on the floor, leaned heavily against the bathroom wall while he rummaged around in her vanity, found a washcloth and ran it under cold water.

"This doesn't look too good, little girl." He hunkered down in front of her, pressed the cool, wet compress to her forehead. Worry darkened his eyes. "What's going on with you?"

"I'm fine…I'm…fine now."

"Yeah." He brushed a stray fall of hair back from her face. "And I'm the Easter bunny. Now give."

She swallowed. Leaning her head against the wall, she avoided his gently probing gaze that demanded she come across with the straight story. "Just leave me alone."

After a long look, he stood, his eyes narrowing dangerously. "Yeah, like that's going to happen. Now come on. Let's get you up. We're going to the emergency room."

She shook her head slowly, catering to her nausea. "I don't need to see a doctor."

"Then tell me," he demanded. "Tell me what the hell is going on here."

Too weary and suddenly too needy to battle him or the damning tears that blurred her vision, she gave up the fight. "What's going on..." she swallowed the thick knot of pain then confessed what she'd been denied the chance to share with Nate. "What's going on is that I'm pregnant."

A long, echoing moment filled the tiny room before his breath mated with the stunned silence of comprehension. He swallowed hard, looked away, then met her gaze with a compassion that broke her. "Oh, Lauren."

The tears overflowed then, slow and hot and too heavy to hold inside.

"It's not fair." She covered her face with her hands and hid from his pitying eyes. But when he dropped to one knee in front of her and touched a hand to her face, his gentleness destroyed her.

She couldn't help it. She leaned into his touch, needing it so much more now than she needed to fight it.

"It's...it's so not fair. Nate...Nate wanted a baby so badly. And...and now that I'm finally able to give him one...he...he'll never know. He'll never know."

He eased down beside her on the cold tile floor, pulled her onto his lap. She couldn't do anything but let him. Let him hold her close. Let him stroke her hair and give her permission to finally be weak when she had tried for so long to be strong.

"Shhh," he murmured over and over against her

temple. "Shush…. It'll be all right. I promise. I promise, somehow, I'll make it be all right."

And because he made it easy, and because she needed to so badly, for the first time since Nate died, she gave herself a moment to believe. Even knowing it was a lie, even knowing it was Mark who held her—Mark, who would run before he'd stay—she clung to him and to the absurd and desperate belief that he would keep his promise. That somehow, he would make everything all right.

# Three

---

Seeing her again, holding her—that's all it took to remind me I'd lost something that had never been mine to lose.
—Excerpt from Mark Remington's journal

**M**ark knew from experience that sometimes, in the dark, it didn't matter whose arms held you. All that mattered was being held. It was all that mattered to Lauren now. And it mattered enough that she stopped hating him long enough to give in to the weight of exhaustion.

He tightened his arms around her and, on a heavy breath, let his head fall back against the bathroom wall. Let his eyes drift shut.

He may have had enough to drink tonight to knock a sailor on his ass, but he was stone-cold sober now. His right leg had fallen asleep. The tile floor was cold and hard against his hip. And still he held her—and wondered where in the hell he went from here.

Pregnant. With Nathan's baby.

A fresh wave of grief swamped him. Guilt was quick to follow. Lauren was right. It wasn't fair.

News flash. Life wasn't fair. Life wasn't just. If there was any justice, Nate would be the one holding his wife and looking forward to the birth of their child.

And trash like him would be pushing up daisies and out of everyone's hair.

Lauren stirred restlessly, and it occurred to him that she might be as uncomfortable as he was, curled up on his lap and wedged between the tub and the wall.

"Honey, come on, let's get you to bed."

She murmured drowsily and snuggled closer, her arm fastening around his neck like he was the one thing on earth she had left to cling to. And while he knew it wasn't really him she was reaching for, something that had been cold for a long time warmed by slow degrees inside him.

"Okay," he whispered along with the kiss he allowed himself to press to the top of her head, "we stay for just a little while longer."

For just a little while longer he could touch the

silk of her hair, smell the warm, woman scent of her skin, feel the slow, heavy beat of her heart against his chest and pretend it was really him that she needed.

Indulgence, however, had a price. Holding her like this stirred memories he had buried seven long years before Nate's death.

He stared grimly at the tiled floor and for the first time since it had happened, let himself remember, made himself recall every detail of the night that never should have happened....

It was the eve of Lauren and Nate's wedding. Mark had never seen Lauren more glowing. Or more exhausted. She was running on nerves and teetering on the brink of tipsy as she sat shotgun beside him in his convertible. The wind whipped her long, sun-streaked blond hair around her face as they careened down the coast highway at breakneck speed.

The night air held the lingering warmth of a July sun and California heat as he steered the low-slung black sports car off the freeway and onto a beachfront access road.

She shrieked when they hit a pothole that sent them airborne before they hit the asphalt again with a bone-jarring jolt. He laughed out loud, and then she was laughing with him as he roared out onto the beach and skidded to a stop that sent twin rooster tails of sand flying in their wake.

Cutting the motor and the lights, he faced her as he slung his right arm over the seat back. "Now— you can officially consider yourself kidnapped."

"You are outrageous." Her eyes danced at the promise of mischief in his even as she sputtered, then gave in and laughed again, a throaty, delicious sound.

Telling himself that the warmth spreading through his gut was only because he was glad to see her loosening up, he twisted around to the backseat to snag a worn blanket and the bottle of champagne he'd filched from the wedding re- hearsal dinner a little over an hour ago. Shoulder- ing open the car door, he unfolded his long length from the seat and slammed the door behind him.

"Don't put a guy down just because he's taking his role seriously. As the groom's brother and best man, I have obligations. You wouldn't think of having the wedding without a rehearsal, right? Right?" he persisted and earned a grudging but grinning confirmation.

"Okay. Then what's so strange about practicing the abduction of the bride? I don't want to botch tradition and since I'll only get one shot at it, I want to do it right.

"Besides," he added, whipping his hair back from his forehead and grinning with a total lack of repentance, "it's your last night as a single woman—who better to spend it with than me? I'm best man in more ways than one, you know." He wiggled his brows, which had her rolling her pretty brown eyes, exactly the response he'd been playing for.

He knew her well. Sometimes too well. He knew how to make her laugh—just like she knew when he was up to no good. Or when he wasn't fit company. The first moment she'd cast those caring eyes his way, he'd known she was someone important in his life. She'd been all of eight years old. He'd been ten. He'd started falling in love with her way back then, even though he'd known nothing could ever come from it.

She was, after all, a McKenzie, born into the perfect middle-class American family. He'd been born into hell. She'd never been exposed to the kind of life he'd endured before coming to live with the Remingtons through social services. Somehow, they'd connected anyway. And even though they rarely saw each other since he'd started building his name as a contender on the Nascar circuit a few years ago, slipping back into their friendship felt as natural as easing into a pair of comfortable old shoes.

It was because they had a history. And they had trust. She'd always accepted him for what he was. Accepted that his traditional way of handling conflict had been to run as far and as fast as he could go. Just like she'd always known where to look for him—and how to quietly tolerate his silences and his rebellions even when she hadn't understood them.

And now she was marrying his brother.

That was good. That was fine. He loved Nate. And Nate was what she needed. Nate could make her happy.

But it was Mark who understood her. After seeing her tension tonight, he'd understood her need to escape—if only for a few hours—the pressure and crush of the last-minute details leading up to the wedding ceremony tomorrow.

"Come on." Wrestling with his booty, he rounded the car and opened her door. "Let's make this worth the effort."

With only token resistance, she let him coax her out of the car. "Nate's going to wonder where I am."

"Let him wonder." With the moon smiling down, he spread the blanket over the sand. "He'll have the rest of his life to keep track of you. Tonight," he plopped down, patting the empty space at his side, "it's just you and me, kid."

With a sigh that told them both she'd accepted her fate, she sat down on the blanket. Her smile grew huge when he gave a lusty whoop as the cork went flying and the effervescent wine bubbled over.

"One of these days, your total disregard for rules is going to land you in deep trouble."

"Never happen," he assured her as he handed

her an overflowing crystal flute—one of two he'd lifted, along with the champagne, from the restaurant.

"And your bad-boy looks aren't always going to bail you out," she teased, falling back on an old dig that earned her a good-natured sneer.

"They aren't going to get me the most beautiful bride this city has ever seen, either." He expelled an elaborate and theatrical sigh. "Bested by big bro again. It's a damn hard pill to swallow."

There had never been any question that it would be Nate that she would marry. He'd always been the one. She'd confessed to Mark once that Nate made her think of the flickering fire in a hearth, warm, mellow, enfolding. His kindness, his steady, self-assured ways, were representative of everything she'd ever wanted and loved.

In contrast, Mark knew that his wildness and greed for speed frightened her as much as it puzzled her. Just as she thought of Nate as a hearth fire, when pressed, she'd confessed that she thought of Mark as a flash fire, scorching, volatile, unpredictable. Dangerous. Too hot to handle and too much trouble to even try. He'd never been for her. She knew it. So did he. He'd never in a million years be good enough for a woman like Lauren.

Her perfect grin flashed in the moonlight as he lifted his glass in invitation for her to join him.

"Now drink, little girl. I consider it my personal responsibility to make sure all your wild oats are sown and out of your system before poor ol' Nate is shackled to you for the rest of his natural life.''

"That's me,'' she said with a studied grimace. "The old ball and chain.''

He shared her smile, then, serious suddenly, touched his glass to hers. "Be happy, Lauren. And make him happy, too.''

The gentle chime of fine crystal rang to the steady accompaniment of slow-rolling breakers. Tears misted her eyes before she nodded, drank deeply, then turned her gaze toward the horizon and the ebb and flow of the tide.

The moon was rising full and yellow over the ocean. The breeze was a gentle caress, lightly laced with salt spray and summer. This wasn't the first time the two of them had escaped from the rest of the world to this very spot. They'd spent endless days on the beach. They were comfortable with each other in a way that neither had ever questioned.

He knew she didn't question being with him now. It had always been her nature to confide in him. He sensed that tonight of all nights, with the champagne to prompt her, a depletion of nervous energy to let down her guard, and the comfort and reassurance of their past to settle her, she was about to confess something that was eating at her.

He didn't have to wait long for the words to tumble out in a rush.

"Would you believe me if I told you I was a little scared?"

She wouldn't look at him. She stared into her glass instead, then toward the wash of waves to shore. He searched her moon-kissed profile, acutely aware of what he saw there. Hesitation and doubt. Neither trait was common to the Lauren he knew.

He was aware of something else too—a sudden tensing in his own long-legged sprawl as he lay on his side on the blanket. Ankles crossed, his weight propped on one elbow, he feigned a lazy enjoyment of the taste and the effect of the champagne.

Beside him, she sat with her ankles crossed, the slight bow of her slim shoulders punctuating the extent of her sudden unease.

He was silent for a time before deciding to press her into confessing. Snaking his forearm around her neck, he gently forced her to her back on the blanket and lorded over her. "All right, kid. Tell me what this is all about. What are we scared of?"

She bit her lower lip, cut him a quick, trapped look, then gave it a go. "You're going to have a little trouble with this.... *I'm* having a little trouble with this." She stopped, swallowed, gave a quick shake of her head. "Don't laugh."

Brows creased, he willed her to continue. "I'm not laughing."

Again, she slid her gaze to his. Again, she

looked quickly away. "I'm worried about the wedding night."

He greeted her declaration with a silence that shouted puzzlement and shock. If she hadn't been so serious, he'd have laughed at the stark admission.

Finally, he found his voice. "You mean...?"

She drew a deep breath and let it out. "I mean we've never...well...we've just never." She sliced him a sharp look. "So help me, Mark, if you dare laugh at me, I swear I'll find a way to make you pay."

Her threat sailed right over his head. "Man." He continued to stare, disbelief muddying his powers of reason—and tact. "Nate's either made of steel or he's an idiot." Brows furrowed, he searched her face as if seeing her for the first time. "Hey. You're not frigid or anything like that are you?"

Her reaction was knee-jerk and immediate. "You insensitive jerk!" She lunged upright, bumping heads in her scramble to get away from him. "Damn you! Damn you for—"

"For what? For putting voice to something you've been afraid to think, let alone say?" he sputtered, wincing at the ache in his head even as he wrestled her to her back again and pinned her beneath him.

"Hey...hey," he murmured more gently.

She gave up the struggle but turned her face away.

"Oh, no. None of that." With a tenderness that brought tears to her eyes for the second time that night, he turned her face back to his, stroked wisps of pale hair back from her temple. "Friends?" he prompted with a hesitant smile.

She let out a deep breath. "Probably not."

He smiled, gave her a moment to settle. "I'm sorry. I'm sorry, okay? And you're right. That was a rotten thing to say. It's just...you took me off guard, you know? You've always talked kind of big. I guess I just took it for granted that you and Nate...well, that you were lovers." He smiled again, searched her eyes with understanding and a hint of mischief. "It's not like you're sweet sixteen."

Both Lauren and Nate had graduated from UCLA last week. Nate had signed on with an advertising firm and Lauren had accepted a teaching position in Frisco where they'd already rented an apartment. In this day and age, a twenty-two-year old virgin was as rare as a summer without sun. Still, he should have known she would hold out for the man she loved.

He watched her carefully until she shrugged.

"You're his brother. I thought maybe he'd said something to you about...about...me. About... us."

"Contrary to popular belief, guys are pretty tight-lipped about the special ones." He touched a hand to her hair. "And you've always been that."

"Special or...undesirable?" A creeping sense of panic undercut her attempt to steady her voice.

"What if I don't appeal to him on a physical level?" she blurted out as if she'd bottled up that particular fear for so long it simply burst free.

He laughed uneasily at the frustration in her voice. "Baby, a man would have to be dead or in a coma not to respond to you."

"Well, you don't," she shot back, unaware of how pouty she sounded. "You don't respond to me...that way."

He scowled before recovering. "That's different," he said defensively, then cupping her chin in his palm, stroked his thumb across her jaw and skated out on some very thin ice. "Kissing you would be like kissing my sister."

Wrong answer, he realized when her crestfallen expression told him that the champagne and the humiliation were taking a toll on her ego. It needed shoring up, fast. Before he could do anything about it, she fired another volley.

"You just said a man would have to be dead not to respond to me—yet I do nothing for you."

"Honey..." he chose his words with care. "I didn't say that."

*"Kissing your sister?"*

His fingers clamped tighter around her jaw and

held her fast. "It was a figure of speech, okay? You're a beautiful, desirable woman. Don't think I haven't noticed."

She considered that, then shook her head, a wild panic filling her eyes. "Then what if it's me? What if what you said is true? What if I'm fri—"

He shushed her with a gentle finger to her lips. His touch was meant to silence. His touch was meant to assure. It ended up being something more. Something he had never expected to share with her. Something he hadn't been prepared for.

The night became very still. He was acutely aware of the fullness of her breast pressed to his chest, of the heat of her body connecting with his, the contrast of cool sand beneath his hip.

With an electric leap of his heart, he realized that after years of making himself see her like a sister, he was letting himself see her differently now. He was seeing her clearly. And he knew she was aware of his sudden turn of thoughts—that she might have been aware of them even before he was.

"Lauren…" His voice was gruff. Her eyes were smoky and very, very dark as he wrestled with a way to deal with the uneasy tension coiling between them and an admission that had come way too late. "Honey, please. Please don't look at me that way."

He could have ended it then. He *should* have ended it then. One word would have done it. It should have been so easy. But it wasn't easy and he could no more stop what had been set so unexpectedly in motion than he could stop looking at her.

In her eyes, he saw her fear that she wasn't what a man needed in a woman—and saw that she trusted him to give her a reason to make that fear go away. He knew what she saw in his. It was longing and wonder and a reckless need that increased by the moment.

Made bold by that need, made careless by her uncertainty, he skimmed the tip of his finger across her lower lip, met her pleading gaze with searching eyes and a suddenly hammering heart.

His eyes apologized, spoke of confusion and regret and a hopeless sense of desperation even as his mouth descended.

It was a whisper of a kiss, a prayer that offered her the chance to stop him, a plea that begged her to do anything but.

He blamed it on the mix of wine and urgency and the immediate press of desire that lured them past reason, far beyond responsibility. He blamed it on the need that that gentle brush of lips kindled, scattering pieces of his common sense to the wind.

She whimpered low in her throat…a silken plea…an extension of trust, then arched against him to welcome him home.

Her response shattered what was left of his control. He was stunned by the rush of it. Compelled by the hot, insistent want of it. And in the end, he was lured by the unyielding need of it that blurred the line drawn by reason and obliterated the definition of wrong.

He whispered her name as his mouth claimed hers, this time to take, not parry, to plunder, not plea. Bracketing her face with the breadth of his palm, he held her still for an assault that was at once savage and tender, an uncompromising demand nudged into action by greed.

He'd expected resistance, but she surrendered completely, became everything he asked her to be. In this moment she was his, and nothing was going to stop him from laying claim.

His tongue was a restless invader, promising an introduction to the passion she should have known with his brother but had discovered, instead, with him.

Even as she clung to him in a hopeless bid to shut out the guilt, he blocked everything but her taste. A taste he'd craved for what seemed like forever.

He groaned, a desperate sound, and tangled a hand in her hair. With an insistent tongue, he probed again, demanding that she open for him…again…then dipped possessively inside when she obeyed.

His fingers found bare flesh between crop top and skirt. Summer clothes and her trusting soul proved scant barrier for skin that was heated and muscle that was tense as he moved over her and dragged the kiss even deeper.

His blood had turned to fire. Molten. Liquid. Flowing. Desire was a drug, tempered only by the power she suddenly held over him. She came alive in his arms, filling him with an edgy expectancy that hovered just outside his grasp.

She shivered, arched her back as he cruised his lips from hers and tracked hot, open-mouthed kisses down her throat to taste more of her. Sensual woman. Yearning. Vulnerable.

Time and place lost meaning. Guilt and remorse were fleeting thoughts, out of sync, out of rhythm with the assault of sensations too honest to deny.

"I want...Mark..." her breath feathered sweetly hot against his skin, a whispered caress. "I want..."

The sound of her voice, needy, trusting, pleading crashed in on him like a tide slamming a rock-strewn shore. With a ragged groan, he raised his head, his face suddenly contorted with anguish, his eyes glazed with desperation.

"Lauren," he whispered hoarsely, each word stretched and wrapped tight around pain, as ecstasy and the agony of reality collided on the down side of desire. "We can't...we can't do this."

Reality rode in on a guilt-ridden wind, slapping him back to the moment and the woman and the magnitude of what they had been about to do.

She had become utterly still beneath him, withdrawing from him emotionally even before she slowly pushed him away. The guilt they'd both been ignoring had a good grip on them now. So did a stunning awareness that if he hadn't stopped it, she would have let it happen.

He threw himself to his back beside her, ground the flats of his palms over his eyes. "What...what the hell just happened?"

Even as he asked, he knew. The years of wanting, the years of denying, the years of pretending he didn't love her and accepting that he couldn't have her had broken down his restraint like a car crashing a guard rail at one hundred miles an hour. And now he was left to deal with the wreckage.

More than innocence had just been lost between them. More than guilt had just been bred by the realization that he had been about to betray a man they both loved—that in essence, he had already betrayed him by starting what, even now, his body ached to finish.

Without looking each other in the eye, they rose, gathered the blanket. Without words, they made the trip back to the city. He wanted to say something...something to set things right...something to explain. But the convertible had barely rolled to a stop in front of her parents' house when she shoved open the door, ran up the walk, and slipped inside.

For a long moment he sat there, wrestling with

the urge to run after her. But the urge to run away was stronger.

He'd been eight the first time he'd run from the squalor of the projects and his mother's bruising fists. He'd been ten when the Remingtons had taken him in off the streets. Made him their son. Made him Nate's brother. Even then, even after they'd given him his first real home, his first real reason to trust, he'd answered that call to run. Many times. As he wanted to answer it now.

He jerked the car into gear and peeled away from the curb.

When he finally came home that night, what sleep he got was fleeting. The dreams he dreamed tangled love with betrayal, dishonor with trust. Discovery with the aching irony of regret.

He'd come from trash, he'd always be trash and he'd just flown his true colors like a filthy, ragged flag. Nate was his brother.

What had he done?

The next day, he watched from a distance as, with violet smudges beneath her eyes that makeup couldn't quite conceal, Lauren went through all the motions of a vibrantly happy bride. Looking anywhere but at him, she smiled for friends and family, posed for the camera—all without ever meeting the silent questions in his eyes.

Between them was a stunning and shameful secret. Between them was a man they loved and a commitment she meant to keep. Worst of all, between them was the flame of passion that against reason and resolve, still burned.

At eight o'clock that night, framed by candle-light, soft music, and the purity of white lace, he watched her walk down an aisle strewn with rose petals. In a church full of family and friends, on a night that should have been the happiest of her life, she became his brother's wife. And Mark became the other man.

Keeping a trust that came too late, holding a faith her silence begged him to save, a sorry excuse for the best man looked on, his love for the bride and his love for the groom twisted around guilt, confusion and shame....

Lauren stirred against him, the sweet warmth of her body and the cold tile of the bathroom floor bringing Mark back to the present with a lagging jolt.

He stared at the wall, shifted his hip. A thousand needles of pain shot down his leg as the blood raced its way back through his veins. Scrubbing a hand across his jaw, he tried to make sense of how things had gotten so out of hand that night. The night he'd betrayed his brother.

It was supposed to have been a lark. He'd had fun, not destruction in mind. When he'd pulled Lauren into his arms it had been to offer reassurance, not to screw up her life.

Or Nate's.

Nate. *I didn't mean to love her, buddy. Not then. Not now.*

Yet, as he sat there on the floor with Lauren sleeping in his arms, he accepted the truth he'd tried to muddy over the years with everything from the speed of the track to booze to women.

He still loved her. He had always loved her.

He'd spent seven years trying to run away from the sad, sweet knowledge. Seven years denying it. Seven years aching with it.

Now finally, he was holding her again and she was still as out of reach as she'd ever been—because of who he was, because of what he was, and because she had more than enough reason to hate him.

And then, there was always the rest of the story. Once she knew that, once she knew the whole truth about him, she'd hate him even more.

# Four

She didn't want me there. I kept telling my-
self that would make it easier to walk away.
I was wrong.
   —Excerpt from Mark Remington's journal

Lauren woke to a soft, warm breeze and dappled
sunlight dancing through the open blinds of her
bedroom window. She stirred and stretched, feeling wonderfully rested. From downstairs, the soft
strains of something bluesy and full-bodied drifted
up to the bedroom, mingling with the sensory
aroma of coffee and—she sniffed and her stomach
growled—bacon.

Nice. A soft smile tugged at the corners of her mouth as she rolled to her side, hugged her pillow and burrowed into the covers for one last indulgent moment of this sweet, familiar, summertime peace.

It crept up on her slowly. That unwelcome sense of confusion—then the all-too-edgy awakening of reality. This wasn't a lazy Sunday morning with Nate.

Nate was gone.

She was alone.

No, not alone, she realized as a prickle of awareness warned her she had company.

Rolling slowly to her back, she stared for a moment at the ceiling. Then she turned her head on the pillow and looked toward the last man she'd ever expected to see standing in her bedroom doorway.

"G'mornin'."

Mark's gruff, velvet-and-sandpaper voice matched the dark stubble on his jaw as he stood there, one shoulder propped against the doorjamb. He looked rumpled and a little ragged in the same jeans and T-shirt as he'd had on last night. And he looked like a man any woman would fantasize about having in her bed.

She averted her gaze and resumed her blank-eyed study of the ceiling.

Only the soft creak of the polished oak floor beneath his shifting feet relayed that he'd reacted to her silent rejection of anything and everything he was—and everything he wasn't.

He wasn't Nate. He wasn't the man she needed. She told herself she didn't want him here, didn't want him looking at her with shadows of loneliness in his eyes that echoed those in her own.

"I made breakfast," he said, from the doorway. "It's warming in the oven when you feel up to coming downstairs."

It was on the tip of her tongue to tell him to go away. That she didn't want his breakfast. She didn't want anything to do with him.

But she'd been alone for what felt like so long. And while he was the last person she wanted to fill that horrible, spiraling void, he was the one who had shown up at her door. He was the one who had refused to budge when she'd managed to push everyone else away.

He was the one who had held her in the night.

The shame she felt for giving in to that weakness hit like a physical blow. When she looked toward the door again to make sure he understood, he was gone.

She was alone again.

Against all her resolve, she felt too keenly the hollow ache his absence created.

It was almost ten-thirty when Lauren walked into the kitchen. At least she has some of her color back, Mark thought as she sat down at the round oak table and let him pour her a cup of coffee. Her cheeks weren't exactly pink, but the chalky pallor was gone. Her hands, however, were anything but steady as she reached for the coffee cup. It rattled softly against the saucer.

She'd showered, washed her hair, dressed in navy shorts and a matching T-shirt. He didn't let himself think about how she'd looked a little while ago waking up by slow, drowsy degrees in that bed. Didn't let himself think of her sweet woman warmth, the fullness of her breasts straining against the soft cotton of her sleep shirt, the golden silk of her hair spilled across the pillow. About lying with her through the night in his brother's bed.

He thought instead of the 9:00 a.m. call he'd intercepted before the shrill ring of the phone could wake her.

A part of him wished to hell he'd let the damn thing ring. Before that call, he could have, in a stretch, chalked her condition up to grief and to the difficulty of dealing with her pregnancy alone. He could have, with little effect on his conscience, reported back to her parents and his that she simply needed a little more time. He could have waltzed right back to Sunrise Ranch, his heart bruised but still intact, confident in the knowledge that they would have given her another week, tops, then converged on her like a horde of guardian angels and healed her hurts with their love and their happiness about the baby. And, through them, he would have fulfilled his promise to make everything all right.

The call and its implications, however, changed everything. There was no walking away now. Now he had a whole new set of questions. Questions he didn't want to ask because he suspected the answers would drag him deeper into her life—where he wasn't welcome—and into a confrontation she wasn't ready to face, at least not without nourishment.

Snagging a hot-mitt, he removed a plate from the oven and set it in front of her. Crisp bacon, toast and a vegetable and cheese omelet spilled over the sides of the dinner plate. A large glass of milk and a small glass of orange juice rounded out the meal he'd packed as full of protein and calcium and natural vitamins as he knew how.

"Eat," he ordered and sat across from her with his arms folded over his chest.

She stared at the overflowing plate, then at him. "I'm not a football team."

Ah, he thought with a measure of relief. There, at last, was some of the spirit he remembered. A smile hooked one corner of his mouth before he could check it or the gentle teasing that used to be so natural between them.

"Well, you never know if you're going to give birth to a quarterback. Why take a chance? You may be incubating a Heisman candidate there."

She merely blinked, dutifully picked up her

fork—then arched a brow that as good as told him he was not a shepherd and she was not some poor lost little lamb that needed him to herd her.

He wasn't so sure about that, but he conceded the point and picked up the morning paper he'd been reading when she'd entered the kitchen.

For all the good it did him. He couldn't focus on anything but that phone call—and the reality that in the clear light of morning, seven years hadn't changed her—not in the ways he had expected. But then, he really didn't know what he'd expected.

She was older, yes. She'd matured into the beautiful woman that everything about the girl had promised. Her eyes were the same honeyed brown, though the laughter had faded along with the sparkle. There was an understated elegance to her long, slim body now, a fullness to her breasts that even her weight loss and shapeless T-shirt couldn't conceal—and that the distance between darkness and daylight couldn't erase from his mind.

Dawn had been slowly breaking when he'd finally managed to coax her off the bathroom floor and carry her up the stairs to the first bedroom he'd come to. He'd had no doubt that it was hers. Hers and Nate's. And when he'd set her down by the bed and turned back the covers, there'd also been no doubt it was Nate, not him, she was wanting when she'd reached for his hand, clung desperately. *Please...please don't leave me alone.*

She'd been drugged by exhaustion or she would never have let herself ask. He'd known that too as he'd tucked her beneath the covers with a murmured promise to stay.

He'd kicked off his shoes and lain down on top of the spread. She'd turned toward him instinctively in the dark, where his face hadn't mattered but the security of another heart beating in the night had. Just as instinctively, he'd opened his arms to her and let her nestle her cheek against his shoulder.

And there he'd stayed. Staring at nothing. Ignoring his hammering heart. Marking the sweep of time as dawn flowed in muted colors over eggshell walls. Unable to block the resurrected flow of memories of the night, seven years ago, that had changed his life forever.

So, now here they were again—on the light side of a morning that had been as dark as midnight when he'd arrived. He glanced from the newspaper to her plate, not surprised to see she'd barely picked at the food, and wondered if she even remembered that he'd held her in the night.

Aware of her sudden stillness, he lifted his gaze to hers and had his answer.

"Thank you."

Too much emotion swam in her eyes to mistake those two small words as gratitude for something as inconsequential as breakfast.

He could have pushed it. He could have made her say it. Thank you for being here for me.

A small part of him wanted to. A small part of him wanted absolution and an admission that he wasn't the bastard she believed him to be. But since it was the bastard in him that wanted to force the issue, he checked the anger, reined in the urge.

Besides, what was the point? He was everything she thought he was, and none of it good. Everything he'd done the past seven years, everything he'd become, he'd become because he couldn't love his brother and love her and watch them love each other.

That's why he'd run. That's why he'd stayed away.

She hated him because of it. But if he'd stayed he'd have made her into someone she wouldn't have wanted to be. And he would have turned into less of a man in her eyes than he was now.

He drained his coffee mug. Set it down. Stared at nothing as he rubbed a thumb over and over the smooth curve of the handle. What would have been was not at issue here. They needed to talk about that phone call—and about the mountain of bills he'd found in the desk by the phone. For her sake, he'd like her to be the one to initiate the conversation. So he banked his impatience, bided his time.

He rose and grabbed the coffeepot. "How about you?" He filled his mug. "Need a refill?"

When he turned, her eyes were brimming with silent tears.

If this had been last night, he'd have gone to her. He'd have taken her in his arms, offered the strength that her grief and her pregnancy seemed to have leached from her body.

But this was morning and everything was different. Her defenses were back up. And her contempt for him couldn't find the shadows of night to hide in.

Ignoring the punch of pain that knowledge fostered, he leaned his hips against the counter and offered the only thing he thought she truly wanted.

"Do you want me to leave, Lauren?"

She propped her elbows on the table, pushed back her hair with both hands. "What I want is for everything to go back to what it was. I want Nate back. I want my life back." It was barely a whisper but it shouted her heartache as she lifted her head, slumped back in the chair and looked past him, focused on nothing. "But that's not going to happen, is it?"

They both weighed the silence of his answer for what it was. Nothing was ever going to be the same again.

"How far along are you?"

She hesitated a moment before answering. "Just a little over three months."

"Have you seen a doctor?" he asked, as much out of concern as to distract her.

She stared at the glass of milk, and as if recognizing her responsibility, brought it to her lips. "Yes."

Again, his silent stare was as effective as a question.

"And yes, I'm taking care of myself. I'm taking care of the baby. Morning sickness is not a new development on the medical scene."

Her drawn features relayed that more than the normal symptoms of pregnancy were taking a toll. Still, he didn't press her.

"I take it you haven't told the folks."

She didn't answer for a moment, then confessed with a shake of her head. "I want to be a little stronger—physically—before I tell them. If they saw me now, they'd—"

"—care for you? Coddle you?"

She set down the glass. "Smother me."

It hurt to see this side of her. The Lauren he remembered was full of life, full of love. The Lauren he remembered was strong and smiled.

"And that would be so bad?" he asked gently, thinking that a little coddling, a little loving attention was just what she needed right now.

She thought for a long moment before responding. When she did, he realized she was extending a trust she was reluctant to share—especially with him.

"They don't need any more pain. Not my parents. Not yours. I...I just need a little more time to pull myself together.''

He sipped his coffee, considering her. ''Has it occurred to you that distancing yourself might be more painful for them than letting them help you through this?''

Accusing eyes shot to his. ''I can't believe that you, of all people, just said that.''

He clenched his jaw. Okay. So he'd been the invisible man for the past seven years. So she hated him for it. She thought he'd left because he didn't give a damn. She thought he'd forgotten where he was loved, that he didn't care who he'd hurt by walking out of their lives without so much as a long look back.

She was wrong. But this was not the time to try to make her understand. This wasn't about him. It was about her.

''It might help them too, Lauren, if they could help you. If they knew about the baby.''

''I know that,'' she admitted as guilt swept over her face like a shadow. She reached for the milk again, ran a thumbnail over the round of the glass. ''I know. And I will tell them—both my folks and yours. But it has to be in my time. It has to be on my terms.''

Hanging between them was the knowledge that one phone call from him would bring both the Remingtons and the McKenzies to her side like a swarm of hovering, loving midwives.

"Please...please give me the chance to tell them when I'm ready."

Her expressive brown eyes relayed much more than pride. He saw everything from an acute sense of vulnerability, a reluctant pleading, distrust of his motives, secrets she had yet to share. Secrets he wished he'd never discovered.

What the hell am I doing here? The question rammed through his mind for the hundredth time since he'd pulled up in front of the house. She doesn't want me here. Yet she needs me—at least she needs someone.

She needs Nate. But Nate was gone and he was a damn poor substitute.

He shoved away from the table, raked a hand through his hair as an overpowering urge to jump in his car and drive as far and as fast as it could take him danced through his blood like fire. Hell. It was what she wanted. It was definitely what she expected. It had been his plan of action since the first time his old lady had laid into him with a belt. Even after he'd come to live with the Remingtons, even after they'd given him the only stability and love he'd ever known and adopted him, he couldn't let himself trust what he'd been conditioned since birth to believe he didn't deserve. Even then, he'd felt that urge to run.

Yet here he stood, looking out the kitchen window at an empty bird feeder and wondering who was going to be around to fill it for her. Who was going to be around to do all the things Nate used to do? Who was going to fix the mess Nate had left her in?

Without a word, he walked to the kitchen door and slipped outside. The day was bright and clear. The yard needed mowing. A flower garden nestled in the corner of the lot needed weeding.

And he needed to get the hell out of San Francisco and back to Sunrise.

Lauren wasn't sure how long she sat at the kitchen table. She didn't want to acknowledge the flicker of curiosity about what Mark was doing outside. It didn't matter that he was here—or why. It just mattered that he left. And he would leave. He always did.

He'd done his duty. He'd checked on her. Now he could report back to her parents any and all of what he'd found out. At least she'd limited her disclosures to news about the baby. He didn't know the rest of it.

*The rest of it.*

The rest of it scared her to death.

Fresh tears welled in her eyes. Nate. How did you let this happen to us? How did you let this happen to your child?

She touched her palm to the very slight swell of her abdomen and wondered, as the panic sucked her under, what she was going to do.

The sound of the garden-shed door opening and

closing shifted her attention to the man outside in her yard. Why didn't he leave? And why wasn't she more anxious to have him gone?

Rising slowly, she stacked their breakfast plates in the dishwasher and stole a covert glance outside. She hadn't pictured Mark as the domestic type. Didn't have a clue why he'd been puttering around in her backyard for what the clock told her was the better part of an hour. He'd refilled the bird feeders. He'd tinkered with the mower, weeded her lilies. Now he had a pair of hedge shears in hand and was frowning at her honeysuckle.

She didn't know how she felt about that. She knew how she wanted to feel and it wasn't this sense of comfort, this false sense of being cared for, of being protected. For one thing, Mark wasn't capable of offering any of those things. For another, as vulnerable as she felt right now, she didn't want to accept them from him.

Yet there he was. He was down on his haunches now, scratching the neighbor's cat, Tigger, behind the ears, then coaxing him gently out of the lilies so he wouldn't break down a tender stalk.

She was moving toward the back door before she had time to think about the slow spreading warmth his gentleness fostered. Then she was outside, sitting on the bottom porch step. The sun burned warm on her shoulders. Tigger spotted her and came trotting, his tail flying high. Lavishly content and purring on her lap, he arched when she buried her fingers in his luxuriant fur. All the while, her gaze kept straying back to the broad shoulders and muscular arms straining beneath the T-shirt as Mark attacked the bushes.

He was so sinfully beautiful. It almost hurt to look at him. Sweat had trickled down his temples and spiked the dark blond hair at his nape by the time he stood back, swiped a forearm across his forehead and studied the results of his work.

He shifted his weight to one hip as she watched him, the action surprisingly like Nate's. It reminded her that when the Remingtons had first taken in Mark as a foster child before adopting him, he'd mimicked everything Nate had done. He'd walked like Nate, talked like Nate. Otherwise, it was only by coincidence that they were both tall, athletically built blonds. The similarities ended there. Nate had been unassumingly handsome while Mark was strikingly so.

It wasn't so much their physical appearance that differentiated them as it was their attitudes. Attitudes that in Nate's case had been ingrained with loving care since birth, while Mark hadn't known anything but anger and fear until the Remingtons had taken him away from that horror.

Nate had been quiet—almost retiring—confident and comfortable with himself. Mark had never been comfortable, and he couldn't help begging to be the center of attention. Even as a child he'd been the first one into the pool, the last one still out at night; the first to play for a smile, the last to end a fight. And the first one to run when the security the Remingtons offered, but that he'd never been able to fully trust, was threatened.

Now she was the one feeling threatened. Now, as never before, she understood the urge to run.

He turned to pick up a rake and sweep up the clippings. He didn't say anything when he saw her sitting there, just went back to work. If he was curious about when she'd joined him, he didn't show it. A bigger puzzle was why had she come looking for him? And why did she sit in silence and let him make his mark on the garden she and Nate had planted together?

The garden, like the house, had been a labor of love. And it was one more element in her life that she would soon lose forever. That inevitable certainty hung like the cloud that suddenly blocked the sun, casting more shadows on a life that was slipping slowly out of her grasp.

"I'm going to miss this place." She was as surprised that she'd spoken the words out loud as she was by the serrated edge to her voice.

She'd surprised Mark too. He stopped raking. Turning slowly, he met her eyes with a look that relayed he didn't think he'd heard her correctly.

"You're not staying here?" he asked carefully.

She set Tigger aside, clasped her hands around her knees and wished she'd thought before speaking. She'd invited his speculation with her recklessness. And now she had to come up with an explanation. Instead of confessing that she couldn't afford to keep the house, she told the other half of the truth. "This was…this was our place. Mine and Nate's. I…I don't want to stay here alone."

She had his complete attention now.

"Where will you go?" The question was soft but intent.

She tugged at a weed growing in a crack between the step and sidewalk. "I don't know. I'll find an apartment, I guess. Closer to the school."

In less than a week she was due to start workshops in preparation for the new school year. Facing a classroom full of eager eleven-year-olds didn't hold the same appeal as it had in the past. Her life's passion had always been teaching, yet even the prospect of acquainting herself with this year's lesson plans couldn't lift her spirits.

"Nate had insurance, right?"

Not looking at him, she rose slowly, walked to her lilies, touched a finger to a silken white petal.

"Don't tell me he didn't have insurance."

"Our finances are none of your business."

Hard eyes made his point. He wasn't backing away from this.

"He had insurance, okay? Everything's fine," she lied, too quickly, too defensively.

One hand wrapped around the rake handle, the other on his hip, he pierced her with a look. "Then why is your friendly banker calling to demand money?''

She spun away so fast the blood drained from her head in a dizzying rush. She swayed, felt a strong hand on her arm, the other at her back to steady her.

When her balance returned, she shrugged away from his hold, her eyes accusing. ''You answered my phone?''

Mark swore softly. So much for avoiding this confrontation. So much for ignoring it and going on his merry way. The nerve he'd hit was so raw she wasn't even capable of fumbling for an explanation. It must be even worse than he'd thought.

''You needed to sleep, so I caught it before it could wake you.'' He refused to defend himself, but figured she was entitled to an explanation. ''Someone named Bruce from First National is very anxious to talk to you about your mortgage—among other things. I told him we'd get back in touch.''

The color that anger had painted in her cheeks drained to chalk. ''You had no right to interfere.''

He set the rake aside, crossed his arms over his chest. ''Then you'll probably think I was out of line looking through your desk too. Lauren—you could start a bonfire with all those bills.''

It was painful to watch her lose her composure. More painful to watch anger bleed into defeat.

''Lauren, what the hell happened?''

Her silence spoke of a tragic pride and an un-
failing loyalty to Nate.

As much as he'd loved his brother, Mark was
so angry with him at this moment, he had to clench
his jaw to keep from spouting his rage. Nate had
to have screwed up royally to leave her in this
mess. How could that have happened? Mark had
always been the screw-up, not Nate.

And how could he, of all people, pose that particular question? Things change. People change.
And like him, it appeared that Nate had also
strayed from the man he'd wanted to be.

So don't be calling the kettle black, son, he told
himself around a rush of shame. The life he'd lived
before he'd left the glitz and glamour of the racing
circuit had been indulgent and hollow. Just like the
women he'd known. Women who moved in and
out of his bed like seasons, women who had
wanted something he couldn't give. Women who
weren't Lauren, could never be Lauren. Just like
he could never be the man she would need.

Her thinly veiled contempt reminded him with
cutting clarity that she hated him—for transgres-
sions too grievous to forgive, for mistakes too huge
to rectify. Yet it seemed that he wasn't the only
one who had let her down.

He was, however, the only one here. Solid flesh
and a handy target on which she could vent her
anger, even though it appeared that Nate was the
one who had committed the biggest sin against her.

"What happened?" he repeated softly.

Just as softly, she gave up. "I don't know." She wrapped her arms protectively around herself and met his eyes with a quiet desperation that ripped him apart. "I...honestly don't know."

# Five

The press had often tagged me a hero. Now,
more than ever, I know I'd never been anyone's hero, especially not Lauren's.
  —Excerpt from Mark Remington's journal

**P**rompted by the single, renegade, Boy Scout gene
he'd been allotted that constantly demanded he
"be prepared," Mark had thrown a duffel into the
trunk before he'd left the Sierras and Sunrise
Ranch. Leaving Lauren in the garden to pull herself together, he retrieved it, showered, shaved and
changed into clean jeans and T-shirt.

She was waiting for him in the kitchen when he

came downstairs. While he didn't intend to cater
to it, he was glad to see a stubborn pride had relit
the fire in her eyes. Clearly, she'd regrouped and
had outlined an agenda that didn't include him.

Just as clearly, he intended to follow his own
plan of action.

"Sit." He pulled out a kitchen chair for her.
"It's time to sort this out."

"Now would probably be a good time to remind
you that this is none of your business."

He was so glad to see a little of her spunk return,
he was almost sorry he couldn't oblige her and
knuckle under to it. Instead, he tossed a fistful of
"past due" bills onto the table between them, then
held up a hand to stall her automatic protest.

"Nate and I weren't brothers by blood. That's a
biological fact I can't change. But he was a brother
to me in every way that counted. And the baby is
my family. That makes it my business."

While she didn't speak, she effectively relayed
her resentment with a cold glare. He understood.
More than not wanting his interference, she wanted
to handle this on her own. Well, that just wasn't
going to happen. She could freeze hell over with
her eyes if she wanted to. Until he had a handle
on this, he wasn't budging.

"Now, sit Lauren. We're going to deal with this,
and we're going to do it now."

By the end of the day, he felt like the neighborhood bully. But he'd needed answers and he'd

been determined to get them even if it meant dragging them out of a woman who was both emotionally and financially broken and valiantly trying to
deny it.

Now he had the information—sad as it was. She
hadn't lied about the insurance. Nate had been covered. The trouble was, he'd borrowed against it.
Not only was there no payout, there was an out-
standing debt that needed to be repaid.

"The driver of the other car?"

She'd huddled a little further into herself then
quietly answered his question. "It was his third
offense, OWI. No insurance, no income, no money
coming from that front—only a small consolation
that he's behind bars and won't be a threat to anyone else for some time."

Though he hated to make her do it, they visited
the bank that afternoon—and things got even
worse. She was pale and shaken when they returned to the house after their meeting. Mark
wasn't feeling too solid himself as he watched her
collapse on the sofa, lean back and stare, with a
glazed look, at nothing.

He cupped his nape, swore softly into the silence
the shock had created. What they'd found out from
a loan officer was that Nate had borrowed heavily
against everything they owned—and against many
things they didn't—to invest in some long shots
that hadn't paid off. With that knee-buckling news,
the color her agitation had heightened earlier in the

day had drained from her face. When the banker had gone on to place a dollar figure on the debt, he'd staggered them both.

"Please," she pleaded, as Mark paced to the bar, poured a shot of brandy, and tossed it down. "Please don't tell my parents—or yours. I don't want them to know. Not until I figure out what to do. I've already given them enough cause for worry."

Mark considered pouring himself another shot. Hell, the worry was just beginning. Instead, he walked away from the bar, working hard to contain his anger with his brother who was dead and unable to defend himself. "You really had no idea of the financial trouble he was in?"

She shook her head. "Not until the bills started coming. Nate handled all the finances. He paid the bills, made the investments."

It was the investments, as it turned out, that accounted for the bulk of their debt. Nate had overextended, ridden with too many hunches that hadn't panned out.

Mark dragged a hand over his jaw. "I don't understand. He was always so level-headed."

A look so forlorn, so condemning stole across her face that his heart kicked him hard in the sternum. "What?"

She looked away.

"What?" he demanded again when she refused to meet his eyes. Her silence fed a dawning, damning conclusion. She'd lied to him earlier. She knew exactly why this had happened. "Lauren—?"

"What does it matter now?" she all but shouted as she rose and paced to the window. "He's gone. Nothing is going to change that."

Her evasiveness only multiplied his suspicions, mushroomed the sense of guilt. She was hiding something. Something that had put her on an edge so sharp, she needed a target. Nothing suggested it was a coincidence that he just happened to be handy.

"This has something to do with me, doesn't it?"

Looking cornered and edgy, she shook her head. "Just leave it alone." Folding her arms across her breasts, she hugged herself as if she were chilled to the bone.

Her eyes pleaded with him to back off. His gut wouldn't let him.

"Tell me."

She paced restlessly to the other side of the room.

"Dammit, Lauren."

"All right. All right!" She whirled on him, her eyes wild. "He was jealous of you, okay?" she blurted out, then the locks opened and a flood of anger poured out. "Is that what you wanted to hear? He loved you and yet...he was jealous of you," she said more softly.

She met his stunned gaze, shook her head. "Not just of your racing success even though it was so very hard to ignore it, Mark. For years we couldn't read a paper or a magazine or even watch the news without seeing your face.''

She cupped her elbows in her palms. ''It hurt him. It hurt him that he wasn't important enough to you to pick up the phone and call—just to let him know you were okay. To share a big win with him so he could be happy for you. Instead, he had to watch it all through the media—the media who adored you no matter what you did.

''And it ate at him,'' she continued, regret and helplessness shadowing her tone. ''It ate at him that he wasn't able to give me the kind of financial security that you had.''

He listened to her words in a numbed shock. Nate, solid, steady Nate, the brother he'd worshiped for his values and ideals, had been jealous of him? Him? The biggest screwup who ever breathed? So jealous that he'd risked his future and Lauren's on some get-rich-quick schemes that had left her destitute?

''You were a hero to him,'' she said, pleading for an understanding that added acid to the burn. ''And he felt diminished because of it.''

A weariness unlike any he'd ever known pressed down like a boulder. ''I've never been anybody's hero.''

''Then why are you here?'' she demanded, shooting past passive resistance to an accusation that burned in each word. "Why are you here, if it isn't because you want to play hero?"

She raised a hand, palm up, shook her head. "Now, Mark? Now, after all these years you want to be the good guy?" Tears of anger, of pain, of injustice welled, spilled over.

"Well, it's too late. Nate's gone and it's too late to change anything." She shoved the hair away from her face, sank down on the sofa, defeated, empty, exhausted. "Damn you," she whispered. "Damn you for thinking you can come back here and make a difference."

Her defeat fed his. That's not what he'd thought. That's not why he'd come. Yet he had nothing to say to her as she challenged in one breath and condemned in the other.

"You can't just decide to pay a little penance for turning your back on Nate and cutting yourself off from everyone who cared about you."

He understood her anger. And he was tired of hurting her, of seeing her hurting, but unexpectedly her anger fueled his, hard and fast and too swift to bank. She'd brought up the past? Fine. She could damn well deal with it.

"What did you want me to do?"

Her head came up.

He challenged point-blank. "Did you want me to stay here so that every day you could be reminded of what happened that night?"

That night. That night when he'd held her and she'd come apart in his arms.

"Nothing happened!" she cried, too vehemently to make the denial anything but a lie. She turned away, whispered in a way that suggested she'd often repeated the same words over the years as if to convince herself. "Nothing. Happened."

Drawing a bracing breath, she squared her shoulders with a determination that told him what he'd already known. He wasn't the only one who had suffered over what they'd almost done that night on the beach. "I was a good wife. I loved him."

Her poignant declaration was sadly defensive. With a weary breath, he gave up the fight he'd never had any intention of starting. "I loved him too. You can accept it or not, but that's why I left. And it's why I stayed away."

Silence, as weighted as her debt, hung between them. Guilt, still begging for justice, tightened its unforgiving grip.

God, what a mess. He wished he'd never come here. He wished he'd come sooner. He wished he knew what the hell to do to make things right.

And wishing wasn't going to make anything happen. Hell. She was probably right. Maybe she'd nailed what this was all about.

*You want to be a hero? Now after all these years?*

Maybe he felt that for once in his life, he had

to do something right in her eyes. And whether she could see it or not, she needed rescuing more than anyone he'd ever known.

And yes, dammit, he wanted to be the one to rescue her.

So you can make her love you?

Sick. He was sick. Her husband was dead. His brother was dead.

He dragged in a deep breath. Let it out. No matter what he would give to make it otherwise, he couldn't change the fact that Nate was gone. He couldn't bring him back. Not for himself. Not for Lauren. Not for the baby. And he could never set things right with Nate.

He could never set things right with her.

But he could do something else.

The idea hit hard and fast, the solution presented itself with a sudden clarity that untangled all the doubts and righted several wrongs. He knew exactly what he had to do. Just as he accepted that what he was about to suggest could only be accomplished if he took brutal and total advantage of Lauren's vulnerability.

And he knew better than to dwell on the certainty that she would probably hate him even more before this was all over.


"You can't be serious?"

More than disbelief clouded Lauren's eyes as she sat at the kitchen table an hour later, a glass of milk in her hand. Denial coupled with resistance to reject the offer he'd just made. He'd expected no less, but he wasn't going to let it sway him.

Her plate was filled with a pasta salad that he had made while he'd honed his thoughts into a proposition he thought would salvage her pride and solve her problem.

Emotionally, she hadn't yet recovered from Nate's death. Physically, her pregnancy wasn't at risk, but she was tired. It didn't take a trained eye to see that worrying and coping with her financial dilemma alone had drained her of her vibrant strength, made her afraid for the child she carried. So for the past half hour he'd been laying it all out for her. He'd pulled every trick out of the bag he could think of.

He wanted her at Sunrise where he would know she was taking care of herself and the baby. He wanted to pay off the debts Nate had racked up. Even her contempt for him, however, took a back seat to her pride. It was her pride, he tried to cater to. So he eased the way with justification for what he was suggesting, keeping his voice steady, talking her up and down the spectrum, getting her used to the possibilities.

He'd thrown out the notion that this was a two-sided sword, that she would be helping him out too. His books were a mess. She could get them back in order. It was a ruse. She'd seen through it, and yet he sensed her soften toward him as if she realized how carefully he was trying to temper the blow to her pride.

"Your folks miss you. So do mine. They've missed you since you moved to Frisco. I know they've always wished you'd consider moving back to Southern California to be closer to them. And now it would mean so much to them if both you and the baby were nearer.

"You know I'm right about your job, too."

With a look, she conceded that point. As a teacher it would be easy for her to get out of her contract. Someone was always waiting in the wings to fill a position.

"After the baby's born, if you still want to teach, you stand an excellent chance of finding another position—closer to your folks—and mine."

Yes, he had all the answers. Still, her eyes told him she felt trapped and without options. Her silence relayed every doubt, every cell of her body resisting.

He knew exactly how to break her down.

All of his life he'd run when the going had gotten too tough. In the projects, he'd run from a hard hand and a shame he'd never understood. Distrustful of the Remingtons' kindness, afraid to let himself believe, he'd still run every chance he'd gotten, every time he'd felt threatened. As a man, he'd run from the woman he couldn't have, from the brother he couldn't bear to watch her love. Hell, he'd even walked away from a career and success that few men could rival because he was tired of looking for a peace he could never find in the speed and violence of a sport he'd done little more than hide in.

What mattered now was that he could give something back. He couldn't offer Nate what he'd needed while he was alive, but he could give something to Lauren—peace, financial security, time to recover. In the process, he could give something to Nate's child.

When the silence became so loud he was afraid he'd lost her, he made one final push. "Give it some thought before you dismiss the idea out of hand."

She'd been thinking plenty. Enough to tag a label on his package. "You've wrapped it up all nice and pretty, but the bottom line is that you're asking me to accept your charity."

He met her gaze directly. "What I'm offering isn't charity—and we both know I'm familiar with charity. If not for charity I'd probably be doing fifty to life for God knows what kind of crimes."

He didn't have to see inside her head to know she too was thinking of the life he'd led before the Remingtons had taken him in. He'd never known his biological father. His mother had been a drunk and an addict. He'd lived on the streets, in alleys, in and out of juvenile hall. The Remingtons had given him a home, given him their hearts. Not everyone was as lucky as he'd been—he realized that now.

So, as to charity. Yeah. He knew what it was. And thanks to the Remingtons and this woman whose life was slowly falling apart, he also knew about love. And he knew about family.

Because of both, he was not going to back away this time.

"You actually made so much money racing that you can cover our debts?"

He smiled. In spite of everything, it was still the issue of money that pricked her pride more than anything. More than pride, though, it was money—the lack of it—that threatened her child's future.

"Yeah. I made money racing. I also bankrolled a friend in a new company he started up several years ago. You may have heard of it. Apostle?"

At the mention of the computer software company that was second only to Bill Gates's financial monster, she blinked. "You own a part of Apostle?"

He shrugged. "Only a third."

She sat back, blew a tuft of blond hair from her forehead. "I...I had no idea."

He set his empty plate on the coffee table. "Now you do. And now you know I can do this."

He waited a beat, restated something he thought she could cling to. "Money is not an issue for me, Lauren, but if you want to put a price on it, cash isn't the only currency of value," he said carefully. He was thinking of the sense of satisfaction he would feel knowing she was okay. That the baby was okay.

She was thinking something else.

What little ground he'd gained was lost in the sharp cut of her gaze. The accusation in her eyes was so damning he felt it like a blow.

"What kind of non-monetary currency are you talking about?"

Implications loomed like thunderclouds. Her low opinion of him sliced much deeper than he should have allowed. Like the street fighter he'd once been, he reacted instinctively with a slicing swipe of his own.

"Sex on demand, of course."

She actually gasped.

He closed his eyes. Shook his head. "For God's sake, Lauren. It's me. Remember? I'm the guy who used to camp out in your backyard."

She colored, drew a bracing breath. "I'm sorry. I didn't mean—"

"Yeah, I think you did." He shoved his plate away, rose from the table, his chair scraping loudly against the floor. "And maybe I deserved it, but you know what? Right now I really don't give a damn what you think. Right now, my concern is for the baby."

He paused, settled himself. "I want you at Sunrise so I know you're all right. So I'll know the baby's all right.''

When her hand drifted to the place where Nate's child slept, something inside him snapped. Something inside him hurt, and made him want to hurt back when the absolute rejection in her eyes carved a deep gouge out of his heart.

He curbed the need to strike back, rolled a shoulder and walked away from her to look out the window as her eyes asked questions and demanded answers.

He didn't have any other answers. None she'd want to hear. None he wanted to share. Shoving his hands in his hip pockets, he chose words that would save his pride and give her reason to accept them.

''Give me the chance to make up for things. To be something I haven't been. Nate can't be here. Let me at least look out for you until you're back in a position to look out for yourself.''

When she said nothing, he let out a weary breath. He was done explaining. He wasn't going to offer her his love. She wouldn't want it. Not with her contempt for him as serrated and sharp as a hacksaw. Not with her grief for Nate still so raw and real.

She wouldn't believe him anyway. And why should she? What had he ever done that would make her think he was even capable of that particular emotion?

He'd run away from her, that's what he'd done, but she'd never believed it was because of love.

He shoved his hands in his pockets, leaned back against the counter. His palms were damp when he issued his ultimatum.

"I want an answer in the morning. And I want you to remember—it's either my solution, or you lay it all on the folks. And then you get to live with watching them struggle not only with their disappointment in Nate, but with trying to figure out a way to bail you out."

He wasn't particularly proud of himself. He wasn't even particularly pleased when she didn't tell him to go to hell. After several moments she merely rose and with weary steps, left the room.

He'd never spent a longer night. And he'd never felt such a mix of relief and guilt when she faced him the next morning and with martyred resolution, accepted his offer.

Sunrise. Only the most compelling of reasons could make him leave here. Like the one sitting beside him. As Mark drove his car beneath the ranch's arched gateway and glanced in Lauren's direction, he knew it would be a long time before he'd leave for this amount of time again.

It had taken the better part of two weeks to wrap things up to the point where Lauren had felt marginally comfortable leaving San Francisco.

There was the house. Leaving it had been hard

for her. He'd tried to spare her much of that. When he'd offered to take care of the details, she'd reluctantly accepted. The only things she'd packed were her clothes and a few personal belongings. Everything else would be sold to help pay her debts. On that, she'd insisted.

He'd insisted that she call her parents and ask them to come and see her before they left San Francisco. He'd sat beside her at the kitchen table when she'd told them about the baby, and about her plans to stay with him at Sunrise.

He left her alone with them when both Grace and Bill Mckenzie's eyes became suspiciously red, but not before they expressed their gratitude with a warm hug from Grace and a firm, approving handshake from Bill.

He hadn't done it for gratitude. He'd done it for the woman who now sat beside him, her eyes coaxed back to life by the wonder of Sunrise.

"It's beautiful," she whispered involuntarily as they crested a ridge and her first view of his home stunned her into momentarily forgetting that he'd coerced her into coming here.

Mark fully understood her breathless exclamation. Sunrise had had that effect on him too the first time he'd seen it. Even from the helicopter as the Realtor had flown him over the three-thousand-acre spread two years ago, he'd fallen in love with the gently rolling pastures, the green-on-green foothills, the mountain peaks dusted with powdery snow.

He'd fallen in love with the ranch's history as well, felt regret for the family who'd had to sell out after holding it for generations. He'd made himself a promise to preserve as much of the past as he could for some future generation to remember.

Nate's child was that future generation.

Without another word, he hit the gas and headed down the final mile to home.

Sunrise proved to be a grab bag of surprises that kept Lauren from thinking about the magnitude of the decision she'd made. She was willingly charmed by the rambling, century-old ranch house that had been restored and furnished with as much attention to history as to comfort. The Spanish influence was dominant and deliciously soothing.

Outside, less than fifty yards from the house, she caught glimpses of pristine white barns bordered by flowers and shrubs. Big lumbering dogs lazed in deep-green grass under the shade of broad-limbed trees. Lean-faced cowboys worked sleek paint horses with long leads in round corrals, as mares and foals lolled lazily in the Southern California sun.

Against her resolve not to, she found herself looking forward to exploring this lush and serene territory that Mark called Sunrise, a name that soft-ened his features whenever he said it.

As he led her toward the house, she snagged quick impressions of cool, cream-colored walls made of thick adobe, half-tile roofs the color of ripe apricots, open flagstone courtyards, trellised archways and vining yellow roses. And fountains. There were fountains made of natural rock and glimmering pools everywhere—outside the living-room windows and the kitchen's cozy breakfast nook, beyond the double doors of the small patio off the bedroom he told her would be hers for as long as she had need of it.

She was standing by the bed, wondering how long that would be, taking in the view of garden beyond her window, when she heard Mark behind her.

"This should get you by until the rest of your things are shipped." He set a suitcase on the floor by the door. "You look tired. Why don't you rest for a while? We'll plan on an early dinner—unless you're hungry now."

"No. No, I'm fine," she said as the enormity of what she'd allowed him to talk her into swamped her.

His polite distance was almost more disconcert-ing than if he'd treated her with the sullen silence she had to fight when she spoke with him.

Her life in San Francisco was behind her. All she had left was a host of memories. Her future was a blank slate. It was frightening. It was humbling. Yet being out from under her worry over the debt Nate had left her, was a relief she'd had no intention of feeling.

She met the eyes of the man who had quite literally solved all of her financial problems and tried very hard not to resent him.

"You're right," she said, aware of his silent eyes watching her. "The drive was tiring." It was early afternoon but her pregnancy and the tension had taken a toll on her stamina. "I am tired. A nap is a good idea."

"Rest as long as you like." He started out the door, stopped, turned.

"Welcome to Sunrise, Lauren."

Then he left her to the silence, to her thoughts, to an unanticipated sense of peace she was too exhausted to question.

# Six

Sunrise. I hadn't realized how much I'd missed it. Hadn't fully understood that when I came back, I was coming home.

—Excerpt from Mark Remington's journal

Little whispers woke her. Quiet murmurs hummed on the air with a singing anticipation and drifted into her consciousness like the gentle caress of a soft summer breeze.

Slowly, Lauren opened her eyes. The bedroom was cast in the rosy blush of dusk. Dusk. She must have slept for several hours. When was the last time that happened?

*The night you slept in Mark's arms.*

The answer was both disconcerting and puzzling. For the three months since Nate's death, until Mark had shown up in her life again two weeks ago, she'd caught sleep in short, fretful doses. The nightmare usually woke her. The one where she saw Nate die. Alone. In a fiery crash.

No nightmare wrenched her violently from this nap. Only those sweet little whispers.

Feeling rested, comfortably content, she was smiling and not sure why when she finally willed herself fully awake. A pair of huge round eyes, as soft as velvet, as blue as indigo, peered at her around a bedraggled bouquet of pastel flowers clutched hopefully in a chubby little fist.

Her smile widened involuntarily.

"We didn't think you were gonna wake up," whispered a beautiful flashing-eyed cherub with twin black braids and a missing front tooth.

"Yeah. We thought you'd sleep 'til tomorrow." A face that mirrored the flower bearer's perfectly, with the exception of the missing tooth, piped up, her animated blue eyes shining with barely banked excitement. "Eddie said we had to be quiet. I picked the flowers. Tonya got to hold 'em 'cause she's the youngest. But I'm the smartest."

"I am too. I'm smart. Sonya just thinks she's smarter 'cause she can talk faster. And I'm only ten minutes younger 'n her. But I weighed the most."

"I cried the loudest. Eddie always says so."

Their opening lines exhausted, the twins stopped, looked at each other as if remembering their mission and murmured in unison, "Did we wake you up?"

Lauren sat up, dazzled by their energy and eager chatter, intrigued by their very presence. Mark hadn't mentioned anything about children at Sunrise. Children with satin black hair and lively blue eyes that laughed and danced and, she realized slowly as she studied them, seemed astonishingly familiar.

Disconcerted, but hopelessly charmed, she took in every detail of their dainty pink outfits. Tiny embroidered roses circled the necklines of their T-shirts and trimmed the pockets and hems of their matching shorts. Their feet, she noticed with a grin, were bare—their dainty little toenails painted soft pink.

"No," she said finally, when she realized they were waiting expectantly for her to answer, "you didn't wake me." She reached for the flowers. "And these are lovely. Thank you—both."

A pair of crooked grins tipped up a corner of each petal-soft mouth. To her delight, Lauren saw that Tonya's grin rose to the left while Sonya's elevated to the right. Sonya's missing tooth was the only thing she could see to differentiate between the two little girls, who she guessed to be about five years old.

"Eddie made supper."

Lauren stretched out the kinks from the lengthy nap. She had another surprise then when she realized she was actually hungry. And still very curious about the twins. Still captivated by their eyes. "That sounds very nice. Who's Eddie?"

"She's our Gramma, only she likes for us to call her Eddie, 'cause it doesn't make her feel so old."

Lauren patted the bed on either side of her. With a little help from her the girls settled at her hips, then gazed up at her, their big blue eyes shining with adoration. Blue eyes, she realized with a dizzying rush, exactly like Mark's.

That's how Mark found her, her head down, holding the wilting flowers as the girls chattered on about baby kittens in the barn and baby horses in the pasture and how they were going to start school next month and ride the school bus and how long was she going to stay and did she really have to rest a lot because she had a baby in her tummy and could they braid her hair?

He leaned a shoulder against the door frame. Crossing his arms over his chest, he watched, too aware that he was indulging himself in the look and the feel of seeing Lauren in his home, comfortable with the girls.

Her hair was mussed and tumbling over one side of her face, her eyes still softly dreamy, her cheeks flushed from sleep. She was smiling at something Sonya had said. Not to be outdone, Tonya de-

manded her attention by wrapping her arms around
Lauren's arm then simply smiling up at her like an
adoring puppy. It was, clearly, a case of love at
first sight—on all three sides.

And he was feeling too mellow about the whole
picture they made and too proprietary about a situation that might be temporary at best.

The smile faded from her eyes when she saw
him standing there. There was pain. There always
was when she looked at him that way—first with
surprise, then with what he wanted to think was
longing, then catching herself, with a cool, distant
disdain.

"I see you've met the welcoming committee,"
he said, not letting her see how one cold look could
affect him.

"Uncle Mark!" the girls cried in unison. They
scrambled off the bed and wrapped themselves
around his legs, both of them chattering at once.
"We were good, just like Eddie said."

"We didn't wake her up. We didn't."

"She woke up all by herself and she likes our
flowers."

Because he'd missed them, because he didn't
want to deal with Lauren's shocked reaction at the
girls' spontaneous cry of "Uncle Mark," to their
giggling delight, he bent over and scooped them
up, settling one twin on each hip. They were
shrieking with laughter by the time he'd nuzzled

tickling kisses on their cheeks. "And where did you get the flowers?"

The giggling stopped. Big eyes grew bigger and just a little bit wary. "Eddie said you wouldn't care if we picked some." This from Sonya, who, as the oldest took the lead as spokesman.

"Yeah," Tonya chimed in from the safety of second fiddle as she patted his face with her hand. "Eddie said."

"Then I guess my vote wouldn't have counted anyway, huh? Besides, you women always do what you want."

"We're not women, Uncle Mark."

"No," Tonya agreed emphatically. "We're just little girls."

Sonya bracketed his jaw with her tiny hands. "Don't you want Lauren to have your flowers, Uncle Mark?"

He looked from her hopeful face to the face of the woman watching him from the bed, her eyes full of questions and unaware of how vulnerable she looked.

"Of course I want her to have the flowers," he said hoarsely, dragging his gaze from her eyes to her mouth and back again. "Sunrise is her home now. That makes the flowers as much hers as mine and yours and Eddie's."

Their gazes held for a long, pensive moment before he turned his attention back to the girls. "Just

make sure you ask Eddie before you pick any
more. You know how she gets.''

Two pairs of eloquently expressive eyes rolled
heavenward in a theatrical, knowing look of long-
suffering. Mark grinned and set them back on the
floor. ''You'd better scoot now. Eddie needs some
help setting the table.''

They took off at a puppy-dog lope leaving him
alone in the doorway. With a casualness he didn't
feel, he leaned negligently against the jamb again,
one knee cocked, and shoved his hands in his hip
pockets. ''I hope they didn't wake you.''

''No,'' she was quick to defend them. ''I was
awake—at least waking up. They're beautiful children.''

A silence clogged with questions settled like
midnight fog. When he'd decided to bring her here,
he'd known that he'd opened up himself and his
life. He'd known she would wonder about Eddie,
about the girls, about his role in their life. He
wasn't sure she was ready for the answers. He
wasn't sure he was ready to give them up.

Regardless, until she cared enough to ask, the
answers would be meaningless anyway. Even then,
what difference would it make? Her future was not
with him.

''Dinner will be ready whenever you are,'' he
said figuring there was time enough to deal with it
all later.

And then he left before he could get too familiar

with the way she looked upon waking. And before he could think any longer about what it would be like to have an invitation to witness that slow, sensual awakening every morning beside her in his bed.

She might have agreed to stay with him, but there was no invitation in her eyes. There never would be. And he understood why.

Yes, he wanted her. Yes, he loved her, but he would never force the issue. She was still grieving for Nate. Even when she got past that, she could never accept him for who and what he really was. And he would never ask her to.

The twins may have been Lauren's first surprise; Eddie, however, was the biggest. And Gramma Eddie didn't have to worry about feeling, or looking old. She was, perhaps, one of the most breathtakingly beautiful women Lauren had ever seen.

She was also one of the most gracious.

"Well, look at you," she greeted Lauren around a huge, polished smile when Lauren walked into the dining room. "Aren't you just the prettiest thing?"

*Pretty* was not a word Lauren would have used to describe herself at this stage of the game. The last three months had taken their toll. She'd lost a good ten to twelve pounds, her complexion was sallow and, at the moment, she still had creases on her blouse and her cheek from her nap.

It wouldn't have mattered, however, if she'd been at her best. Next to Eddie, Michelle Pfeiffer would look like dry toast.

The woman was stunning.

Eddie's long hair, which reached midway down her back, was a riotous mass of springy black curls. Her figure, in ivory raw silk slacks and a jade silk blouse, was straight out of a fashion magazine. And her face—her face was a study in perfection, as flawless as the china spread out on the table.

"You must be famished," Eddie clucked, her perfect, wing-shaped brows drawing together in concern. "Here, now. You just set yourself down and we'll see what we can do about taking the growl out of that tummy."

A soft, guiding hand settled on her arm and steered her to a chair, then squeezed in reassurance.

"Mark, honey, I could use a little help. March on out to the kitchen with me and put those broad shoulders of yours to work." She winked playfully at Lauren who hadn't been able to do anything but absorb in speechless silence.

"Gramma Eddie made soup," Tonya piped up from her seat across the table as Mark obediently followed Eddie into the kitchen.

"Cream of something-good-for us," added Sonya not looking all that enthusiastic. "But if we eat it all we get dessert. You too, Larn," she added with an encouraging smile as she struggled around the pronunciation of Lauren's name.

Lauren returned their bright smiles with one of her own and kept it frozen in place when Mark hipped open the swinging kitchen door, a large soup tureen clutched between his big hands.

"You drop it, darling," Eddie warned, right behind him with a bowl of salad in one hand and a platter of delicate, crustless sandwiches in the other, "and the two of us will be having a serious discussion about your prowess as a real man."

"If I were a real man," he said with a grunt and a good-natured grin as he set the tureen in the middle of the table, "I wouldn't be playing fetch-and-chase to a house full of women."

Eddie only smiled, hugged an arm around his waist and squeezed. It was an action they both looked very comfortable with. "You love it and you know it."

He returned her smile. Lauren smiled too, but it was forced and short as she struggled with an unexpected and troubling sense of exclusion that suddenly swamped her.

"He loves to step and fetch for us," Eddie assured the room at large—and Lauren could see she was right as Eddie turned her cheek for Mark to press a kiss there that was so sweet, so soft, so openly loving that the surprise of it had her looking away.

She recognized yet another involuntary reaction. Jealousy. It was so unexpected and so strong and completely inappropriate. But it was there just the same, as confusing as it was embarrassing.

This was a side of Mark she hadn't expected to see. This was the old Mark—at least shades of the old Mark, the young man who had begun to come into his own, who had begun to trust his worth enough to let down his guard and smile without self-censure, indulge without guarding his back.

She felt uncomfortable watching such an open display of affection when she hadn't yet figured out what the connection was between Mark and Eddie. And the twins. She didn't know how she would feel about finding out that Mark and Eddie were lovers...if they were lovers.

She studied the twins and their gamine faces, their blue eyes so like Mark's. Their hair so black like Eddie's. Uncle Mark. Gramma Eddie.

She didn't know what to think. Didn't want to react—and yet she did, stunned to find that unbidden and unacceptable hint of jealousy still hovering on the edge of her curiosity.

Troubled, she concentrated on her dinner, made polite noises when asked, smiled when it was called for, and told herself it was none of her business.

This wasn't her life. It was Mark's. Or it was, until she and the baby had become a part of it.

The baby. Nate's baby. She couldn't reconcile his loss with where she was, who she was with, what she felt about being here—because she didn't know what she felt. She knew what she should feel. She should feel pressured. Trapped. Compromised.

And yet, none of those emotions troubled her as much as the notion that Eddie and Mark may have made those beautiful children together.

Somehow, she made it through dinner. Alone that night in her room, doubting the wisdom of coming here, weighted by the reality of the debt she owed Mark, dizzied by the uncertainty of her future, she made the only decision she could.

She would get through this. She would rest. She would take care of herself. She would concentrate on the baby. She would not agonize over money she didn't have, or debts she couldn't pay.

She would become an island. She would float, unattached, through the hours, through the days, through the weeks and months. She would survive and somehow make her life her own again.

Neither would she wonder if perhaps Mark had changed. If there was still something of the old Mark who had been her friend. She wouldn't consider what demons had chased him, reshaped him, remade him into the man who had run. That above all, she would remember. The Mark she had known, even the Mark she didn't know, would run. He always had. He always would. And when he did, she'd be alone again.

She would not let herself remember that the man

had once been a boy, frightened and confused, alone and abused. And she wouldn't let herself believe that a part of her still wanted to love him.

For to believe that would be the ultimate betrayal to a husband she had loved—but not enough.

The girls were in bed. Mark had thought the whole house was down for the night when Eddie joined him on the patio with a glass of wine in each hand.

She extended one to him, sat down on a cushioned chair next to his. And said nothing.

He shifted, stared at his glass, stared at the glittering brilliance of the star-packed sky.

"You want to talk about it?" Eddie asked softly.

He looked at her, looked again at the sky. "Nothing to talk about."

Eddie gave a soft snort. "And that, ladies and gentlemen of the jury, is a classic example of acute denial."

Long moments passed before she tried again. "Have you told her about me and the girls?"

He shook his head. "I will. When the time is right."

More silence then her soft voice. "And when is the time going to be right to tell her that you're in love with her?"

He wasn't surprised that she'd read him so easily. Didn't bother to deny it. Did deny the possibility. "Not an option." He tipped back his glass.

"Because?" she prompted gently.

He slumped back in the chair. "Because."

The weariness in that single word encompassed a world of reasons why it could never be. Because of his brother, because he repulsed her, because he wasn't now and could never be the man she needed.

"She watches you. She watches me," Eddie said with a soft smile. "And she's trying to decide if she's jealous."

He scowled. "She's still grieving. She doesn't know what she's thinking. She only knows she hurts. And I'm the last man she'd ever feel the need to be jealous of."

Eddie rose, settled herself on the arm of his chair, dropped a kiss to his brow. His arm came around her waist automatically. "Don't be so sure, darling. Give her some time," she murmured against his hair. "Sometimes, all it takes is time."

They both knew about time. How it could heal. How it could be hell. How it could consume and contain and leave you with nothing but pain. Just like they both knew that time was often the enemy—and sometimes, there wasn't enough time in the world to make things right.


"We've only got one rule at this house," Eddie lectured after issuing a cheerful hello to Lauren the next morning when she walked into the kitchen. "Make yourself at home."

Eddie was standing in sandals and a slim black

swimsuit. Her white fishnet cover-up did little to conceal her voluptuous figure. Lauren felt like a fading violet in her pale lavender blouse and gray slacks.

"The fridge is always stocked, the coffee is always hot." Eddie's smile blossomed over her shoulder as she swung open the refrigerator door. "How are you feeling, honey? Do you want me to make you some breakfast?"

Lauren returned her smile and headed for the coffeepot. "I've got a rule too. You don't have to wait on me. I'll make my own breakfast."

Concern furrowed Eddie's brows. "Mark says you haven't been feeling so hot."

"I'm fine, really. Okay," she conceded, responding to Eddie's doubting silence and unable to resist her kindness. "I'm still dealing with a little morning sickness, but it's getting better. I'll be fine. I'm actually hungry this morning. That's a good sign, right?"

She walked to the refrigerator, found a bowl of fresh fruit and set it out on the counter.

"Well, you just set your own pace and I'm sure you'll be over that nasty business in no time."

The kitchen door opened and Mark walked in. Beneath the brim of a doe-colored Stetson, his scowl was dark and fierce. "What nasty business?"

"Oh, relax, Marshal Dillon." Eddie picked up a bright red beach towel she'd laid across the end of the counter and slipped on a pair of sunglasses. "It's just woman stuff. You wouldn't understand. Just like those little girls aren't going to understand if I don't get out to the pool so they can get in the water. They're about five minutes past their patience limit and I hold out little hope that they aren't already dangling their toes. I don't want to start out their day by scolding them.''

She breezed out the sliding doors, toward the pool that lay glistening in the warm California sun. Lauren made a point of watching Sonya and Tonya as they waited like little angels in their hot pink swimsuits a safe distance from the water.

She didn't let herself look at Mark until she was sure she could absorb the impression he made standing there—tall and tan and smelling pleasantly of hay and horses and leather and sweat.

She'd seen him in jeans and T-shirts, she'd seen pictures of him in his racing gear, in his leather jacket and jaded smile, and, from a distance, in a tailored black suit at Nate's funeral. She'd never seen him in boots and gloves and a well-worn working man's Stetson. She'd never seen him as a cowboy.

He was transformed into someone else she didn't know. Someone who, despite all that had happened, made her skin tingle with sharp little frissons of awareness.

In long, steady strides, he walked across the kitchen's tile floor, his footsteps falling in muted clicks as his boot heels hit the floor. Sweat trickled down his temple, tracked down his cheek under his jaw and made a river trail in the dust coating his neck before disappearing beneath the collar of his blue chambray work shirt. He wiped it away with a brush of his forearm, tugged off his gloves with his teeth then tucked them in the hip pocket of his worn, dusty work jeans.

She was still staring, mesmerized by the transition of all that restless energy into this lean, sinewy grace, when he turned on the tap and shot a glance over his shoulder.

He filled a glass then downed it in one long, thirsty gulp before he turned to her. "How are you feeling? Did you rest?"

Who are you? she wanted to shout. A graphic, lurid picture she'd once seen on a cover of a tabloid flashed in her mind's eye. He'd been laughing, his arms wrapped around a starlet with big hair, a big bust and a very small dress. His hair had been mussed, his face unshaven and they'd appeared to be holding each other up, the bleary look in their eyes more than hinting they'd been partying all night.

She couldn't forget about that side of him. That he'd led a life of decadence, that he'd been a user of people, an abuser of trust. Just because he had brought her here, just because he acted concerned, didn't mean he wasn't everything she'd come to believe he'd been, or that he wouldn't run when the need hit him.

But what was he now? Savior or sinner? And how long before one of his women showed up? There had to be women. A man who looked like Mark would not ever lack for female company. Another flash of memory slashed unbidden, shooting a quick burst of heat through her blood: the weight of his body pressing her into the sand, the hunger of his mouth, the need in his kiss.

She closed her eyes, stunned by the rush of desire a seven-year-old memory could stir, shamed by her body's immediate reaction and by her curiosity about the women who might now litter his life. It was none of her concern what he did.

She looked toward the pool. Toward the children who might be his and the woman who might actually be their mother, and she became angry about what she didn't understand, haunted by what she didn't know. And more determined than ever to distance herself from everything he represented.

"Lauren? Are you all right?"

His voice, the pinched look of concern on his face brought her back. No. She wasn't all right.

"I'm fine."

He refilled his glass, then leaned back against the counter, his brows creased. "Did you sleep—"

"Yes. Yes," she snapped then stopped herself. Restless, she moved to the window. "Yes. I slept. And you have got to quit hovering."

He watched her with quiet eyes.

She focused on the girls splashing in the pool, then on her hands. "I'm sorry. I'm sorry I'm so waspish. I…just need a little time to get used to things."

She pressed a thumb to her lips, faced him. "It…it's not easy being here. It's not easy being dependent on someone…other than myself or Nate."

Mark's voice was full of reason. "I can't pretend to know what you're going through. I can't pretend to say I've been where you've been. I can only ask that you give yourself the chance to simply be here. Sunrise is healing—let it work for you."

Mark wanted to go to her. To hold her close, tell her with the warmth of his body, the strength of his arms that everything would be fine. But that right wasn't his and she wouldn't welcome him anyway.

She was so unyielding, so consumed still by her grief—and by her resistance to him. He watched the stiff set of her shoulders, the tight rise and fall of her breasts. She wasn't happy. She might never be happy again. Yet he felt a relaxing of his own tension just seeing her here. In his house. In his kitchen—as if she belonged.

It hit him then that he'd always imagined her here. It registered from somewhere deep inside that when he'd first seen the house, as he'd walked through the rooms, testing the fit, he'd always seen her with him. By his side. In his bed. As he'd always wanted her.

Even while she was married to his brother.

He didn't like to think about what kind of a man that made him.

For so many years, Nate had been the only brother he'd known. The Remingtons the only family he'd ever had. He looked toward the pool as the sound of the twins' little-girl laughter danced into the silence of the morning. Well, he had more now. He had the girls. He had Eddie. And though he'd badgered her into it, he had Lauren.

He didn't want to think about what that made him either.

"I have to get back to the horses," he said abruptly. "Whatever you're up to doing—just do it. Make yourself at home. After dinner, I'll give you a guided tour if you like."

She turned to him, a study in defiant pride. "You said something about having some work for me to do."

He smiled. "My office has been in a mess for so long, a few more days of neglect won't hurt."

"I need to do something—"

"—to earn your keep? Is that what you were going to say? Don't worry," he said, giving her a toehold on the pride she needed to recover. "When you see my office, you'll know just how good a deal I got.''

He downed his second glass of water in another long gulp, reached into the fridge to grab a soda and headed toward the door. ''Just rest for a few days, okay? Humor me. And humor the girls and Eddie. They could all use the diversion another female mind can provide.''

Then he left, wishing she could trust him enough, wishing she cared enough to ask about the girls, about Eddie, about how they fit into his life here at Sunrise. Accepting, grimly, that it was cowardice more than his pride that would keep him from filling in the blanks for her.

# Seven

She's healing. I can see it in her eyes. She
smiles now. The girls are responsible for that.
And Eddie. They've given her a reason to
focus on something other than her own pain.
—Excerpt from Mark Remington's journal

It would be wise, Lauren decided, to take Mark
up on his offer to make herself at home. For the
baby's sake, she needed to find some sense of
peace. So she sat in the shade of a green-and-white
striped table umbrella and praised the girls for their
daring deeds in the shallow end of the pool as a
patient Eddie gently encouraged them to hold their
breath under water.

They really were remarkably beautiful children, these two precious little girls that Eddie clearly loved—as did Mark. The question that had plagued her since she'd awakened to those expressive blue eyes always hovered close to the surface. It wasn't any of her business, but she couldn't look at those eyes without wondering if Mark was their father, if Eddie was their mother.

If that were true, then it didn't make any sense. It was obvious they both loved them so why would they not want to claim them as their own?

Was it because of Lauren's presence here?

That thought seemed ludicrous. Eddie was a warm, giving woman, but no woman would willingly let another woman trespass on her territory.

She couldn't reason it out. Couldn't imagine a scenario that would fit. And wouldn't ask because she didn't want to let it concern her. So she ignored the niggling little voice of curiosity, promising herself she wouldn't cave in to it.

Later, the girls gave her a tour of the house. It was huge and rambling and warm. She couldn't say exactly why, but the house—from the sun-catching arched windows to the terra-cotta tiles and vaulted ceilings—eased something inside her that had been tense for a very long time. It had to be the house.

As they strolled by a window, she looked toward the barns where Mark worked alongside the wran-

glers and dismissed out of hand that it had anything
to do with him.

The tour, thankfully, excluded Mark's room and
ended at the girls', where her suspicion that pink
was their favorite color was confirmed by the pink-
on-pink decor.

It was a little girl's dream room filled with frilly
icing-pink ruffles, raspberry-pink carpet and everything from dolls to dinosaurs to ducklings filling
the shelves and nestled against barely pink pillow
shams on the twin beds. It made her yearn, with a
bittersweet longing, to know if this child of Nate's
that she carried would be a beautiful little girl or
a precious little boy.

She picked up a pale pink stuffed elephant. Held
it to her breast.

Oh, Nate, I wanted so badly to give you this
child.

Not just because she knew he wanted a baby,
but to make up for that part of herself she'd never
been able to give him in their marriage—just like
Nate had always wanted to give her the wealth that
had eluded him and that Mark had amassed. The
irony was stunning—Nate's search for that wealth
had left her in a position where she had to depend
on his brother for her very existence.

Just before lunch, she walked around the
grounds, careful to keep out of range of the barns
and the corrals where she caught more glimpses of
the cowhands working alongside Mark and the

glistening hides of the spirited paint horses he seemed to handle so well.

Eddie loved to volunteer information but carefully kept it generic.

"Mark raises and trains the horses for show and pleasure riding. It started out as a hobby but turned into a business. You'd think he'd slow down a little now that he has eight hired wranglers on salary, but the horses are a passion for him. He's very active," she added with pride, "and stays involved in each area of their training."

After lunch she did what she had put off for too long. She called Nate's parents to let them know she'd settled in, and to set a date next week for them to visit the ranch. When she hung up the phone, for the first time since Nate had died she was looking forward to seeing them—and to sharing her news about the baby, news that she knew would help them fill the void of Nate's absence.

When she had called them last week to tell them she was moving temporarily to Sunrise, they had accepted the announcement with a calm that should have surprised her, but somehow didn't. Neither her parents nor Nate's were aware of the history between her and Mark. Thanks to Mark, neither would they know about the financial problem Nate had left her with. For that, she was truly grateful. It was hard enough for them to grieve the loss of their child. To try to make sense of what he had done would add unnecessarily to their pain.

The Remingtons were excited by the prospect that her presence at Sunrise might even bring Mark closer to them again. And they were glad that, for the time being, she wasn't alone.

To them, it was a sign she was getting on with her life. The thought filled her with guilt. How could she think about getting on with her life when Nate's had ended?

Exhausted, she napped again, slept like a stone, and awakened—as she had yesterday afternoon and this morning—without the jarring horror of the nightmare. She chose not to question why. Considered it a transition of sorts, like her transition from San Francisco to Sunrise.

When she realized how late in the day it was, she washed her face, ran a brush through her hair and headed for the kitchen to see if she could help Eddie with dinner.

Eddie looked up from setting the table when Lauren walked into the dining room.

"Those little pixies didn't bother you awake again today, did they?"

"No, they didn't. But someone should have. I wanted to help with dinner."

Eddie smiled. "You are always welcome in the kitchen, but there's no need to help. I like to cook and what little bit you eat isn't going to make one ounce of difference in throwing a meal together.

"If you really want to help, though," she added on her way back to the kitchen, "you can round up the troops for me. Mark's already washing up but the girls are outside somewhere.''

She found the twins in the yard engrossed in the braids they were meticulously weaving in each other's hair.

"Larn," they cried happily when they spotted her. Scrambling to their feet, braids forgotten, they each reached for one of her hands.

"Did you see your new garden?" This from Sonya.

"*My* garden?"

"Yeah," Tonya chimed in. "Uncle Mark planted it. Come see."

They led her toward the back of the house where little squares of flower beds broke up the lush green sod like colorful patchwork lap quilts. Tucked back in the shade of an overhang and bordered by a sundial and stepping stones was a plot of freshly turned soil.

"See?" Sonya announced standing proudly by the little patch of earth where green stalks sprouted out of the dirt. "We helped."

"Yeah. Uncle Mark said you would miss your lilies in San Fr'isco, so he brought them with him and planted them for you."

She looked from the girls' smiling faces to the carefully tended soil…then to the man who had just walked around the corner looking for them.

"We showed her the garden you made, Uncle Mark. With her lilies in it."

For the longest moment, all she could do was look at him, at this beautifully sculpted, impossibly enigmatic man who she wanted very badly to resent, who she'd spent the last seven years blaming for sins too numerous to count. And she didn't understand how that man could be the same one who looked a little trapped and marginally uncomfortable that he'd been caught doing something as thoughtful as transplanting her lilies.

He shrugged a shoulder. ''Seemed a shame to leave them behind.''

She just stood there, stunned by his kindness, touched by his sensitivity.

Before she could find the words to thank him, he broke eye contact, honed in on the girls.

''I heard a rumor that there's chocolate cake for anyone who can clean up their plate.''

Sonya let out a big, all-knowing sigh and screwed up her face into a comical grimace. ''Well, you know what that means.''

''Yeah,'' Tonya said with a lusty groan and headed for the house. ''Broccoli. Yuk!''

''Think cake, girls,'' Mark suggested with a grin as he herded them toward the kitchen door. ''It's just a little trade-off.''

''Eddie always has a catch,'' Sonya grumbled.

''No free ride.'' This, from a wise-beyond-her-years Tonya that made Lauren smile.

She followed the parade to the house. And thought about her lily garden. And wondered if there was more to this man than she had allowed herself to see.

Lauren wasn't sure how it happened but somehow a month went by. And then another. Her lilies took root and bloomed. The girls were firmly entrenched in their first year of school. The baby grew healthy and strong inside her as her third trimester grew near. And life, the one she was determined to merely drift through until she found her footing, had taken on a comfortable rhythm, settled into a familiar pattern despite her resolve to remain detached.

Except for trips to town for supplies or to run errands for Eddie, Mark rarely left the ranch. And no women came to stake their claim on him.

She and Eddie generally made the trip to her doctor's appointments together. They went shopping together, too, for everything from groceries to baby things, drawing on funds from what Eddie referred to as the household account.

She tried not to feel anything but joy over the room that would be the nursery and that was fast filling up with everything from crib to receiving blankets. And for the baby's sake, she tried not to let her total dependence on Mark bother her.

It was evening in the Sierras. As he had done every night in the two months since she'd come to Sunrise, Mark had left the house shortly after dinner.

Eddie was reading in the study. Lauren had helped the girls with a school project and now they were watching one of their favorite videos.

Feeling a restlessness that had become too familiar, she walked out to the patio, lifting her face to the west where the day was slowly giving way to dusk.

In the distance, a lone rider crested the ridge. The breadth of his shoulders, the angle of his head identified him as distinctively as a fingerprint. It was disconcerting to realize she could pick Mark out in a crowd, or from this distance and know without question that it was him. Even more disconcerting was the sudden realization that she'd come out here to watch for him.

Reluctantly, she accepted that she watched for him every night. She couldn't say when that had become a part of her daily routine. More importantly, she didn't understand why had it come to feel so essential.

She only knew she was drawn here to silently watch. The stark, surreal beauty of the picture he made riveted her where she stood. Sunset chased him along the leading edge of the horizon, casting both horse and rider in a clean black silhouette against the melon-yellow glow of a rapidly sinking sun. One man alone, made insignificant against the vast, rugged beauty of the Sierras. One man whose loneliness she hadn't wanted to acknowledge, whose needs she would never comprehend.

She turned away, awash with emotions she didn't want to examine. Feelings that she couldn't sort out and that, by their very existence, reminded her that she had not merely drifted through the days as she had planned, had her swimming in a river of uncertainty.

She laid her hands over her growing roundness of abdomen, taking comfort in the steady growth of the child within even as she was mired in yearnings she didn't understand. Yearnings for the man who was gone—and even more now for the man who rode alone.

She went to bed that night—and the nights that followed—unsettled by her discoveries. Night after night, week after week, she would lie for too long in the dark, with the sounds of night settling around her, with knowledge of the other hearts that beat in this house that was now her home.

She'd been at Sunrise almost three months before she finally accepted some gnawing truths.

She wasn't cut out for solitude. She wanted to be a part of a family again. She was weary of living on the edge of those beautiful little girls' lives. By her own choice, she still didn't know any pertinent information. Nor did she know anything about Eddie, other than that she was kind and generous—and if she had ever been Mark's lover.

They weren't lovers now. She was certain of that but not certain why that knowledge gave her such relief. She'd watched them together. There was affection between them, yes. There was a history she'd denied herself access to by refusing to ask what she knew Eddie would gladly tell her. She'd refused to ask because she'd been convinced she didn't want to know. In this case, knowledge was not power: knowledge was weakness. The more she knew, the more she'd want to know—and the more she would be pulled into Mark's life.

She couldn't let herself think about the way she felt when she found Mark watching her—and he did watch her. Just the other night, after dinner, she had sensed his gaze, raised hers to meet it. In the brief, intense moment of contact, she swore she saw longing and hunger and a loneliness that, if she let it, would tear her heart in two. In the next instant, however, his eyes were blank. His quick, reflexive smile indifferent.

She rolled to her side, stared into the dark, and fought a physical desire that confused her, excited her. Shamed her.

How could she think of him that way? How could she look at him while her husband lay dead? How could she want him while she carried Nate's child? Nate's child, who was now less than three months from being born.

But he moved her—his gentleness with the girls, his generosity with his help. His ranch was peopled with individuals—some of whom he'd known through his racing career. They were people, she'd learned from Eddie, who were down on their luck, who needed a place where they could get back on their feet and still keep their pride intact.

Mark gave them that and more. He gave them jobs. He invited them to his dinner table. He gave them their dignity.

Just as he was giving hers back to her.

In the beginning, she hadn't wanted to credit him with kindness. She hadn't wanted to accept that he was a benevolent man. She accepted it now. With that acceptance, came the most difficult fact she'd had to deal with yet.

Even though it hadn't made any sense, even though it was a betrayal to Nate, she really had wanted to believe Mark had brought her here because he wanted her with him. After three months of keeping his polite distance, however, the truth was now obvious. He'd felt obligated to bring her to Sunrise. Duty bound.

She was no different than the rest of the people who'd found refuge at the ranch. She was a person with a problem, and Mark—the man she'd let herself believe was a user of people, an abuser of trust—was a soft touch who couldn't turn away a stray.

She was just one more sad story who was taking advantage of his generosity.

So, no, it wasn't longing she saw in his eyes. It was obligation. Somehow, that grim reality hurt more than the guilt she felt for needing him.

To her shame, she did need him. She needed him

in a way that, no matter how hard she'd tried, she'd never needed Nate. And that was the most difficult truth of them all to face.

Crisp October sunlight shone through the patio doors as Lauren walked toward the kitchen the next morning on stockinged feet. The pale blue cotton maternity sweater that she wore over white leggings felt good against the mild California fall chill.

The sight that met her when she reached the kitchen doorway, however, warmed her as no summer sunshine could.

As quietly as a pregnant mouse, she crossed her arms over the growing mound of her belly and stood, transfixed. Beneath her forearm, the strength of the kick that a healthy, twenty-seven-week-old fetus could deliver made her smile. So did the scene in the kitchen.

The twins sat side by side on the edge of the table. Mark sat on a chair directly in front of them, his brows furrowed in concentration, Tonya's bare foot cupped in the pocket of his big palm. Legs spread wide, his Stetson tipped back on his head, he dipped a brush into a bottle of Hot Panther Pink nail enamel.

"Now hold still, you little wiggle worm or I'll end up painting your nose instead of your toenails. Good Lord, could they *be* any smaller?"

Beside her sister, Sonya twisted a braid in one

hand and cupped her chin in the palm of the other, looking very, very bored. "Hurry up, Uncle Mark. I was supposed to be first."

He grunted as Sonya's legs swung impatiently back and forth. "Yeah, well, if you hadn't had to go pee, you wouldn't have lost your place in line. You snooze, you lose, kid. Now, darn it, Tonya, hold still—look what you made me do."

Tonya rolled her eyes. "Eddie sure is a lot better at this than you are."

"Well then why don't we just wait for Eddie to get back from town?" he groused.

"'Cause then she'll be too busy doin' this or doin' that," Tonya predicted to the nodding agreement of her sister. "And you promised you'd do it, Uncle Mark, 'cause Eddie doesn't have time today."

"Why couldn't this have waited until tomorrow?" Another grumble even as he leaned over those precious little tootsies and with hands the size of bear paws, attempted to carefully and precisely turn her pale nails bright pink.

"Tomorrow she's making jam. And baking pies to put in the freezer for Thanksgiving next month. That's when we're gonna eat a big old fat turkey." Both girls gobbled at the top of their lungs then doubled over in peals of laughter.

Lauren had come upon many scenes of Mark indulging the twins in storytelling or board games in the past few months. She'd seen him tussle and tickle. Once, she'd seen him braid their hair, those strong hands and long fingers taking such gentle care that it had made her heart hitch.

She'd never, however, seen him play pedicurist—and the soft thump of her heart as she watched him told her she wouldn't soon forget it.

Nor would she soon forget the look on his face when he sensed her standing there.

He craned his neck around, turned beet red then returned his attention to the wriggling toes cupped in his palm.

"I don't know how I get myself into these things," he muttered.

Lauren knew. He was a pushover. He'd do anything for the twins. He'd do anything for someone he loved. Including leaving a brother he loved to keep from causing him pain.

It had taken a long time for her to come around to that conclusion. It was taking longer to come to terms with it.

"Okay, you're done."

Mark's voice jolted her back to the moment. He turned Tonya's foot from side to side and blew gently on her toes to dry the polish as he checked out his handiwork.

"Do me now," ordered Sonya, fairly bouncing with her excitement and promptly stuck her foot right under Mark's nose.

He growled, grabbed and bit gently—which sent Sonya into a giggling, squirming squeal that almost knocked Tonya off the table. Mark deftly snagged her, set her right then drew a deep breath.

"What I don't do in the name of women's vanity. Now give me that foot, peewee—and not in my face this time."

More giggles.

"Anybody want juice?" Lauren asked around a grin as she walked to the fridge.

"Me!" both girls chorused.

By the time she'd poured four glasses and found a tray to carry them to the table, all ten of Sonya's toes were the same pretty pink as her sister's.

"Nice," she said when the expression on both pixie faces pressed for approval. And because Mark looked so abused, she couldn't resist. "In my opinion, your Uncle Mark should take over the job from now on."

"Nobody asked your opinion," he muttered but let go of a reluctant grin when she handed him his juice.

The tension had eased between them since she'd settled in at the ranch. Gradually, time had marked a new beginning, an easiness between them that was at once familiar and new, despite the underlying remoteness each of them strove to keep in place.

"You should do Larn's toes now, Uncle Mark."

"Yeah," Tonya echoed. "Uncle Mark—make Larn's toes pretty like ours. You'd like that wouldn't you, Larn?"

"Oh." Her gaze flicked to his, found him watching, waiting to see what she was going to say. "Well, as much as I'd like to have pretty toes, Uncle Mark looks tired to me. Aren't you tired, Uncle Mark?" The question demanded an affirmative answer.

Uncle Mark, however, sat back in his chair, the beginnings of a sparkle lighting his eyes. She hadn't seen that look for a while, but she recognized it just the same. It was a pure, ornery, dance-with-the-devil dare.

"Oh, I'm not so tired," he said innocently, then challenged her with those dancing eyes as he tipped up his glass for a long, slow swallow. "I've probably got one more toe job left in me."

Something about the way he watched her, his blue eyes full of mischief, his crooked smile teasing, took her to a place and time where everything had once been special and right between them. And she forgot, for the moment that she had kept guard of her feelings around him. Forgot that no matter how he sugarcoated it, she was still one of his charity cases. Forgot, even, why she'd thought there was still some reason to keep her distance.

"Well," she said, considering the dare and not stopping to question why, "with such a charming incitement, how could I refuse?"

Never taking his gaze from hers, he hooked a chair with his boot, dragging it away from the table. The invitation to sit down and play this out was as clear as the California sky.

A slow, challenging smile split his perfect face as he picked up the bottle of polish and slowly shook it. "I'm ready when you are...Larn," he added, in a drawling imitation of the girl's pronunciation of her name.

She hesitated, belatedly thinking better of the idea. He may be ready. She wasn't sure she was. This would involve touching. Something she tried not to think about at all costs.

But she sat, because it was expected. And then shifted, slowly lifting her left foot. She jumped with a tight, jittery smile when he reached out and caught her heel in his hand.

She hadn't yet found the breath she'd lost at his first touch when an unexpected rush of heat chased like fire from his hand up her leg. When he tugged off her sock, she had to bite her lower lip to keep from moaning.

Oblivious to what was happening to her, the twins chattered from their perch on the table beside her chair. She heard their voices. Even made out some of the words. But she didn't comprehend anything they said. It took all of her concentration to keep from sliding off the chair in a pregnant puddle as one big hand, so gentle with the girls, so sensually tender with her, slowly massaged the arch of her foot.

Her toes curled and she heard a soft moan. Hers,

evidently, because his head came up. Beneath the shadowed brim of his hat, his brows creased. "Did I hurt you?"

"N-no. I—I um...I'm just a little...ticklish," she managed as he lowered his head again and lifted her foot toward his lap.

She stifled another groan when he eased it down on his thigh.

Oh, Lord.

Sensory impressions swamped her, each one stronger than the next as his callused hands guided her bare foot into position on top of his thigh.

Heat. Soft, worn denim. Hard, solid muscle. Sinew and bone.

She didn't know where to look as he unscrewed the lid of the nail-polish bottle. She wasn't even sure she could breathe. And she'd never, ever dreamed that the touch of a man's hands on her foot could create such an onslaught of dizzying sensations.

Slow, spreading heat sizzled in delicious warm licks from her arch, up the length of her leg to the tips of her breasts before spiraling slowly to her feminine core.

The shock of her arousal paralyzed her. The fact of it stunned her. So swiftly, he'd brought her to this needy edge. With the innocent touch of his hand. With the blatant fact of his masculinity. With the memory of one kiss, one forbidden summer kiss on a windswept beach a long, long time ago.

She closed her eyes to block the visual impact. It only made things worse. Her imagination played devil's advocate, drawing mental pictures of his hands moving further up her leg. Drifting, lingering along her inner thigh. Cruising with studied awe over the firm roundness of her belly. Caressing, with aching wonder and infinite care, the fullness of her breasts. And finding, with a slow, steady hand and a lover's touch, the heat and the heart of what made her a woman.

Strong, capable and sure, he caressed her. Until…until…

"You're done."

Her eyes snapped open. She blinked once, twice, her eyes slow to focus.

"Lauren?"

His grip on her ankle tightened as he lifted her bare foot with her shocking-pink toenails from the warmth of his thigh and set it carefully on the floor.

"Lauren?" Concern furrowed his brows. "Are you all right?"

"F…fine. I'm fine." She scrambled to her feet, the extra weight of the baby throwing her off balance.

He shot up and grabbed her arm. Eyes wild, she met his dark look—and knew in a heartbeat why he didn't ask her what was wrong.

Her flushed cheeks were a dead giveaway. He knew his way around women too well to mistake her distress for anything but what it was. Arousal. Primitive and hot.

She tore her gaze away. "I—I've...got to...got to go."

"But Larn, Uncle Mark's got to do your other foot. Silly, you can't leave yet."

She touched a hand to Sonya's cheek. "Later, sweetie. We—we can finish later."

And then she walked. As fast and as far away from the kitchen and the man as her five pink toes and one stockinged foot could take her.

# Eight

I made a big mistake with her. And she's too
lost to see the obvious. It's not me she's
wanting. If I'm half the man I need to be, I'll
make sure she understands.
—Excerpt from Mark Remington's journal

She had wanted him.

For two nights Mark had lain in bed with the
moon and his mood his only company and thought
back to that afternoon. For two nights, he'd burned
over what had happened. The way she had burned
for him.

He rolled to his back, punched the pillow beneath his head, restless, even now, feeling the heat of her physical response like a brand.

And what now? Was she lying awake aching for him the way he ached for her? Or did she hate him for unleashing those yearnings?

What difference does it make, Remington? Nothing can ever come from it. It never should have happened in the first place.

What the hell had he been thinking? He'd pushed her into a situation she hadn't been up to dealing with. He'd made a bad call because she'd seemed so relaxed that morning—smiling at the girls, easy with him. She'd let her guard down. Joined in the fun. Taken his dare—and then he'd gone too far.

Toenail polish, for God's sake. He threw back the tangled covers, sat up in bed and lowered his head to his hands. And thought of the delicacy of her toes, the slim length of her calf—of the way she'd flushed, of the way she'd trembled. Of the kick in his gut when he'd finally accepted that in that moment she'd wanted him as much as he'd wanted her.

Two days ago.

Grabbing his jeans from the chair by the bed, he dragged them on. Staring out the open window, he scrubbed his hands across his face then shrugged into a shirt. He needed to move.

It was midnight. The sky over Sunrise was clear, but a storm was brewing in the distance. Dark clouds banked thick and heavy and high over the mountains as he slipped out of his room and walked quietly down the hall. Lauren's bedroom door was open. He stopped, debated, looked inside.

Her bed was empty, the door to her patio ajar.

Telling himself it was because he was concerned, he walked inside, crossed directly to the open door and found her outside.

In the soft glow of a quarter moon, in the dark of the night, she stood alone. Like his, her feet were bare. Her white robe was a pristine, dreamlike contrast to the black-on-black shadows and shapes that surrounded her.

She was so tragically beautiful it made his chest hurt. She looked lost and vulnerable and alone. He wanted to take her in his arms, wrap her in his strength until the hurt that drained her of the woman she had been leeched from her body into his and set her heart at ease.

And he wanted to take her to his bed to heal her with his caresses, to prove to her that life remained, that love remained—even if it wasn't with the man she wanted.

He would never be that man. Oh, she might want him physically, but he would never be the man she needed. He could never even come close.

That's why he'd made himself so scarce. He'd worked long hours with the horses, taken long rides before sundown, avoided the office where she labored meticulously to put his books in order.

Until two days ago. That one accidental meeting had undermined every attempt he'd made to avoid exactly what had happened in the kitchen…

Well he could avoid this. He wasn't up to a repeat and he was fairly certain she wasn't either. He turned to leave.

"Don't go," she said so softly he wasn't sure if he'd wished the words or if she'd actually spoken them.

He looked over his shoulder, found her watching him, found her…needing him.

He took one step toward her when he should be taking ten steps away. But something was wrong. He searched her face as a night breeze shaded and shadowed her delicate features in the moonlight. "Are you all right?"

Her smile was slow and sad. She lifted her chin, closed her eyes, gave a quick shake of her head. Her swift, fleeting smile was touched with panic. The flurry of words that followed, was edged with a desperation that her slow, controlled delivery undercut.

"I'm twenty-nine years old and I'm just figuring out that I still don't know what I want. For that matter, I don't know who I am. I think…I think we could safely say that I'm not all right."

She met his eyes in the dark, tried for another smile, gave it up and looked quickly away. He said nothing, gave up on leaving.

"I don't know how I got here." She drew a

shuddering breath and touched her hand to the rough bark of an ornamental tree. "I don't mean here. To Sunrise. But to this point in my life where I don't know what…what part of me to trust anymore."

She lifted a hand, let it drop. "How does that happen? How does the only child of parents who were loving, supportive, gentle people become so lost?"

He waited in silence, devoid of answers, even though he suspected he understood what was happening with her.

She was rethinking things. She was regretting and sorting and trying to make sense of her life. So he kept his silence, sensing that what needed to be said this night would be said by her.

She folded her arms beneath her breasts, tipped her head to stare at a quarter moon the color of aged Swiss cheese. "I grew up in a neighborhood where the grass was green and the trees were old and we played hide and seek after dark without fear of kidnappings or shootings or worse. I was protected my whole life. The only element that wasn't pure Ozzie and Harriet was when the neighbors took in a boy off the streets."

Her blond hair, gilded by moonglow, tumbled down her back, drifted across her shoulders. He watched and waited and wondered how far this was going. Knew, without question, she had reached an impasse of sorts.

"His name was Mark," she said, facing him again, searching his eyes with a thoughtful expectancy that made his heart gallop. "You were a very scary curiosity—and then you became my friend."

Restless, she walked to the fountain, sat down on the edge of concrete and stone, trailed her finger through the water. "I was always intrigued by your wildness. Your quick, slashing temper, the anger that seemed to hover just beneath the surface. I used to lie in the dark and cry for you."

She glanced up, and he felt his gut tighten. He remembered. He remembered that eight-year-old girl with the huge brown eyes, and he remembered that she had been the first person ever to cry for him.

"When my parents told me that you had come from a bad place where you didn't have a father and your mother didn't take care of you, and that sometimes you didn't have food to eat or a warm bed to sleep in or someone to hold you instead of hit you, it made me cry."

He scrubbed his jaw in the mitt of his hand, reliving his life before the Remingtons, remembering her sad eyes staring into his and why he had begun to fall in love with her way back then.

"I remember when I told you that once. That I'd cried for you. You told me you didn't need anyone crying over you. You acted like you were mad at me. It broke my heart. But after a while, you started coming around again. And then we became real friends. And you became Nate's brother.''

He reached above his head, wrapped his fingers around a low-hanging limb of a flowering crab tree loaded with fruit.

''It was a long time ago, Lauren.'' His voice was a hoarse rasp in the velvet softness of the autumn light. But she wasn't listening. She was remembering, and sorting and sifting through memories she was determined to bring back to life.

''You lied for me more than once.'' A soft smile lifted one corner of her mouth. ''Little white lies to keep me out of trouble, but I thought it was about the bravest thing anyone had ever done. You were my friend and you stayed my friend...until the night before I married Nate.''

*Until the night before I married Nate.*

He swallowed back words that seemed shallow and too little and too late.

''I'm still not sure what happened.'' A desperate confusion tightened her voice, made it small with a very real and puzzled reflection. ''We were having fun, letting off some steam. I was grateful you'd gotten me out of there—nervous about the wedding, jumpy with a bad case of bride jitters. That's all it was, I was sure of it.''

She stopped, touched her fingers to her lips. ''But then you kissed me. To make me feel better. And I let you. I...I don't know why. It just happened. Then you wanted to do more than kiss me.''

He swallowed hard, remembered. Remembered her sweet, giving response. Just as he had remembered, almost too late, that she belonged to his brother.

"I wanted it too," she confessed, her voice little more than a penitent whisper. "I told myself it was because you were so sweet and I was worried and that I couldn't stop you. But the truth was, I could have stopped you any time.

"But I liked it. I liked it better than anything Nate and I had ever shared. And that scared me even more."

His heart clogged his chest. He couldn't move.

"So I ran. I ran because I was afraid. I married Nate the next day and I promised to love him and to cherish him, forsaking all others.

"Only," the breathlessness of her words brought his head up, sent his heart hammering. "Only there was always...there was always another. There was always you."

Her eyes swam with unshed tears. He couldn't take any more. "Lauren. Lauren, don't. Don't do this."

But the floodgates were open. And he could see nothing was going to stop the flow of words that now tumbled out like white water over rapids.

"I couldn't forget about you. I couldn't stop thinking about you. I tried." She paused, shook her head. "I tried but during the day...during the night...when Nate and I made love—I thought about you. And I felt like I was betraying you both. Thinking of you. Lying with him.''

He went to her. Drew her into his arms because he couldn't bear to see the haunted look on her face anymore.

She clutched fistfuls of his shirt, buried her face against his throat. ''Sometimes, sometimes I thought if I could just talk to you I could sort it out. I could put it in perspective. But you weren't there. You ran. Like you always ran.''

I'm sorry. I'm sorry. The words swam in his head. Too little. Too late.

''Nate never asked why you left. He didn't ask why sometimes in the night I'd wake up and leave our bed—and think of you. And hate myself.''

Abruptly, she pushed away, as if she'd just now realized she'd turned to him and couldn't let herself. ''I tried to get on with my life. I did everything a good wife does. I made a home with him. I loved him as best as I could. And he loved me without question.''

Her eyes took on a lost look. ''He never asked, but I think he knew. I think deep down, he knew that the reason you never came home, the reason you raced around the country in those cars that could end up killing you, the reason you ran away from your family was so you wouldn't have to face us.

''Sometimes…sometimes there would be a news report and your face would suddenly appear on the

TV. We'd both be spellbound, listening to each word, taking in each detail to see if you were really all right, wondering if you missed us.

"I began to dread those times. Yet, I'd also search the rows of magazines in the grocery store for photos and stories. Even the bad ones that ended up in those tabloids—the ones that showed you with a different woman each week, that chronicled wild parties and hinted at excesses too ugly to contemplate."

He was past defending himself. There *was* no defense. There had been parties. There had been women. There had never been Lauren.

"I'd go home to Nate. And I'd think, how could I still think about you when I had a man like this to love me? Unconditionally."

"Lauren—"

She shook her head, pulled away when he reached for her. "Eventually, I started to hate you."

The truth of her words hit them both hard. "I hated you for the lie you had made of my marriage, for making me want you, when this man—this good, kind man who wanted me, who needed me— had never understood why some nights I would turn away from him in his own bed.

"And now that man is dead." She faced him again, her eyes swimming with tears. "I can never, ever tell him how sorry I am. I can never tell him

I loved him." She touched a hand to her abdomen. "I can never tell him about his child."

A tear spilled over. She swiped it away, then laughed. Harsh, short, bitter. "And now I am dependent on his brother, the man who stood between us in life, for my very existence after his death."

A wind gust cooled Mark's skin, fluttered her gown around her bare feet, molded it to her breasts, the gentle mound of her abdomen. "How do I live with that?"

She balled her hand into a fist, clutched it to her breast. "How do I live with the love I felt for him and know it was never enough? How do I live with the hate I felt for you—hate that was unjustified, unfair—and tell myself it's all right that I'm living under your roof?

"How do I live with the knowledge that it was what I felt for you that drove you away from your family?"

Another short, strangled laugh. This one desperate. "And here I stand, feeling sorry for myself when you were the one who was wronged."

Thunder rumbled in the distance. A rising wind heralded the coming storm even as the first raindrop fell.

"And how do I live with the fact that I still want you?"

The despair in her ragged whisper hung in the air, thick as the storm clouds that all but burst with the weight of their cargo.

Another night, another time, he'd have embraced her confession as he wanted to embrace her. He'd have confessed his own love, promised her forever, taken her to his bed.

On another night.

On this night, however, he knew what drove her—and it wasn't for love or for want of him. It was guilt and sorrow and a void she wanted desperately to fill.

"You don't want me," he said gently, knowing it was true, wishing with everything in him that he was wrong. What would have been wrong was to take advantage of her vulnerability. "You want Nate. You want what you lost."

He wanted to be her cure more than he wanted his next breath. But he wasn't her cure. And he wasn't her hero. He was nobody's hero, and, in time, she would figure that out. "I'm sorry. I'm sorry, but you're not going to find what you need with me."

Her eyes were huge and tortured when she raised her face to his.

"I'm no good for you, Lauren. I was never good for you. I'm not made for the long haul. I think we both know that."

He touched a palm to her face, stroked his thumb along the rise of her cheekbone. "You're tired. Get some sleep. Everything will look different in the morning."

He left her then. He left her, wishing he could

be something he wasn't, knowing it wasn't even a slim possibility.

Mark had been right about one thing. Things did look different in the morning. As Lauren showered, she thought about everything that had been said last night. The one thing that most came to light was that she knew a lot more about Mark now that she'd opened herself up to seeing him through eyes unclouded by unfounded resentment. She also knew a lot more about herself.

It had taken her this long to come to terms with all the questions that had haunted her. She hadn't intended to pour out her deepest feelings to him last night. But just when she'd needed someone, he'd found her outside by herself. And the words had burst out, as if they had been waiting for that moment, for that man to set them free.

She hadn't known how confused she'd been, hadn't been able to pinpoint exactly what it was that ate at her so. She understood more clearly now. The experience had been cathartic, the beginning of a healing of sorts.

She understood now that it was herself she had hated all those years—not Mark. It was her own sins against Nate that had weighed so heavily, not any sins she had perceived to be Mark's.

She was slowly coming to accept those truths. She was slowly coming to forgive herself. She had given Nate all she'd had to give. She'd been a good, faithful wife. And she had loved him as best as she could.

She accepted that now, and that acceptance meant that it didn't hurt quite as much to think about Nate as it used to. The sharp edge was gone, eroded slowly, a little bit at a time. The constant reassurance of the life growing within her held most of the responsibility for that. So did the reality that hers wasn't the only life touched by grief. Mark's parents also knew about loss, yet they carried on. They persevered and made do with visits to Sunrise and their delight over the baby. And Lauren knew now that she, too, would survive.

Yes, Mark had been right. Things did look different in the morning. He was wrong about only one thing.

It *was* him she needed. It *was* him she wanted. Even as she missed Nate, it was Mark she needed to hold her in the night.

It was past midnight when the vet pulled out of the drive. One of Mark's yearlings—an accident waiting to happen—had somehow hooked a hock between two fence rungs. Fortunately, the damage would heal, but he'd needed Doc Turner to stitch up the filly's leg.

Relieved and exhausted, Mark let himself in the back door and headed straight for the shower. For decorum's sake—should one of the girls tippy-toe out of bed in search of a glass of water—after he toweled himself off, he stepped into a pair of clean jeans. Tugging the zipper to half mast, he headed for the kitchen and something to take the hollow bite of hunger from his belly.

He walked through the dark, quiet rooms—and found that he wasn't the only one prowling around in the night again.

His heart slammed inside his chest the moment he saw her. Damn, he'd wanted to avoid another one of these midnight encounters. He couldn't take another one. Not and walk away without doing something they'd both regret later.

But, for a moment, he was riveted where he stood. She was alone in the dark, framed by the patio doors, the lushness of her pregnant body silhouetted in the soft spill of light from a three-quarter moon. Almost seven months pregnant and the sight of her body, starting to grow heavy with child, heated his blood. His sex stirred, heavy, pulsing.

Her breasts were full and ripe, the dark, protruding tips of her nipples clearly defined beneath the thin material of her flowing white nightgown. Her abdomen was gently distended, her hips woman-full, sloping gracefully to the slim curve of her buttocks. Long legs, smooth and sleek, were softly rounded where the top of her thigh met the golden nest of curls that guarded her woman's core.

The strength of his urge to touch her there, to

taste her there, to suckle at the breast that would nourish her child, hit him hard and fast. So hard, so fast, he knew he had to get the hell out of there before he did something unforgivably wrong—or unforgivably right.

He was about to turn and go back to his room when she touched a hand to her lower back, rubbed so gingerly that his blood cooled from arousal to concern in one solid beat.

In two strides he was at her side. "What's wrong?"

"Mark!" Startled, Lauren whipped her head around, then reacted without thought and touched a hand to his arm to steady herself.

Beneath her hand, his bare skin burned. "I—I didn't hear you come in."

"What's wrong?" he demanded again, his voice a hoarse whisper. "Your back—you were rubbing your back."

Lauren carefully lifted her hand away. "It's nothing. Just a little pressure. The baby shifted today."

"And that's normal?"

She forced herself to nod, steady her breathing that suddenly seemed as erratic as her wildly beating heart.

"It all goes with the territory," she whispered as her gaze drifted to his mouth. And lingered. She hadn't been able to think of anything but him since that morning in the kitchen. Or that night, less than a week ago in the garden. "I'm fine. It…it just aches a little."

He was so close. She could see the midnight stubble of his beard, the dampness of night on his skin, feel the heat of his body feed the burgeoning warmth of hers. Breathe in the scent of his skin. Dark. Dangerous.

And then his hand was at the small of her back, gently probing, carefully kneading.

"Here?" The warmth of his fingers and the skill of his touch combined to wring out a little moan of uncompromised pleasure.

"Umm…yes…right…oh, right there. Mark… you don't have to do this." Stunned by the sheer, sensual pleasure that eased one source of pressure and intensified another, she tried to move away.

A warm, firm grip on her arm stayed her. And all the while, he touched her there, just above the base of her spine, expertly pressing, skillfully massaging.

Another soft moan, a shivering breath, and she gave in, let the soothing power of his hands work their magic. Let the need to be touched, to be coaxed, to be lulled grant permission, provide excuses.

"Here…" He turned her to face him.

His hair fell roguishly over his brow as he looked down at her. Moonlight and shadows darkened the rugged planes of his face, shaded the sensual fullness of his mouth, the lean curve of his night-stubbled cheek. She wanted so badly to brush that hair back from his brow, to cup that impossibly square jaw in her palm.

"Lean on me…"

She was helpless.

"Yes…like this," he whispered as she let him gently press her forehead to his chest.

With both arms around her, he worked his fingers in a slow, sensual rhythm up and down the ridge of her spine.

Heaven, was all she could think. What he was doing to her was heaven. And she tried to think innocent thoughts. She tried to think of strained muscle and pressure points and the healing power of touch.

But it had been so long since a man's hands had touched her. So long since she'd sighed at a man's caress. So long since she'd reconciled herself to her need outdistancing his.

She relaxed completely, leaned into him, aware that the pressure had changed. That the need had changed, intensified, grown. The need for him. The need she had denied for so long.

She sighed a little as he held her there, gloriously close, languidly aroused as the neck of her gown slid down her arm, baring a shoulder.

Against her cheek, the steady heart that beat slow and strong escalated to a hard, rapid tattoo. The breath that feathered the bare skin of her shoulder became heated and shallow. His gentle kneading slowed, transitioned with barely a shift in rhythm, became, with unimaginable finesse, a sultry, coaxing caress.

Her breath caught in a thready little hitch as awareness shifted from lazy contentment to a hot, sensual awakening. It was so easy. He made it so easy to give in to him. So natural to give herself over to him. To this beautiful man who painted little girl's toenails and knew how to make big girls moan.

And who proclaimed he wasn't the man she needed.

He brushed his lips across her temple. Once, twice, then groaned into her hair as he clutched the gown at her hips into his fists. Pressed her close.

"This is wrong," he murmured. "This is all wrong for you, Lauren. Tell me...tell me this is wrong."

His whisper was as hoarse and harsh as his hands were gentle. They skimmed from her waist to her hips and pulled her even closer. To feel him. To understand what she did to him. To beg her to come to her senses and go running to her room.

She lifted her hands to his chest, spread her fingers wide, letting him know she wasn't going anywhere.

His erection was huge and hot and strong where it pulsed against the firmness of her belly. Against her jaw, his breath burned, as he nuzzled and nipped, then lowered his mouth to her shoulder.

"Touch me," he groaned, giving up, giving in. "Unless you want me to stop, touch me. Please...please touch me."

She hadn't known she'd been waiting for permission. Hadn't guessed he had this much need. Hadn't thought that her pregnant body could arouse him—or that her heart could beat this fast and not explode or that her legs could still hold her when her knees felt so painfully weak.

And then she wasn't thinking at all. She was feeling. She was indulging. With wonder and awe, with the same necessity as breathing, she skimmed her hands along the washboard leanness of his belly. Caught her breath as she encountered the open waistband of his jeans, the satin-soft tip of his arousal straining above his half-zipped fly.

He groaned and, cupping her face with his hands, took her mouth in a kiss that was as savage as it was tender, as hungry as it was giving.

Breathless, dizzied by the taste of him, and the craving for him that she'd suppressed for years, she let him take her under. Let him back her up against the window, ever gentle yet voraciously greedy as he took her mouth and took her mouth until she felt nothing but the warm wetness of his tongue, the cold, hard glass against her back, his hot, lean strength pressing against her.

"If you don't want this, tell me." He dragged

his mouth along her jaw, savored the slope of her shoulder, bent to take her breast in his mouth through the thin cotton of her gown. "If you don't...tell me," he murmured as he gently laved her tender nipples, cupped their weight in his palm. "Tell me now and I'll stop. But tell me now."

She knotted her hands in his hair, arched against him. "I don't...I don't want you to stop. Please... please don't stop."

He wrenched his mouth away and swept her into his arms. "My bed. I want you in my bed."

They didn't make it to his bed. Hers was closer. And close was what they both needed as he stripped off her gown and laid her down on the moonlight-dusted sheets.

She melted into the bed, watching him through a haze of desire as he peeled off his jeans then eased out full-length beside her.

Beauty didn't begin to cover it. He was long and sleek, leanly muscled, sinewy and strong, his skin a sun-baked bronze, satin smooth, glistening.

She wanted to touch him. To lie with him, skin on skin. Heat on heat. It was a need she'd denied herself for so long it clawed at her.

She lifted a hand, touched it to his stubbled jaw. He turned his face into her palm, covered her hand with his and bit gently. Licked.

She shivered as he guided her hand, wet from his mouth, to his erection. Such heat. Such power pulsed in her hand as she closed her fingers around him, surrounded velvet steel and rubbed her thumb across the glistening tip. He bucked, threw back his head, the cords of his neck taut, his jaw clenched.

And she felt the power even as she gave herself over to it.

With care, he drew her hand away, put it beside her head on the pillow.

"Too much," he murmured as he lowered his head to her breast.

"Too soon. I need to taste you first. I need to touch you..."

He flicked his tongue across her nipple, wringing a needy sound from her before his mouth closed fully around her. With exquisite care, he suckled her sensitive breasts as his fingers caressed and compromised then stole to the hard mound of her abdomen.

"I don't want to hurt you," he whispered, pressing his lips there. "I don't want to hurt the baby."

"You can't. You won't. Oh, Mark..." she dissolved in a mindless moan as his mouth cruised to her hip point then to the crease where hip met thigh. And then lower, to that part of her that pulsed as he had pulsed in her hand.

"Mark..."

"Shhh...let me..."

The heat of his mouth. The hush of his breath. The total selflessness of his giving. She lost herself in it. In the rush. In the roar. In the ride that coaxed her with a wild, intense fury. The release sent her soaring, left her boneless and quivering and helplessly sobbing his name.

She was still coming down when he pressed a kiss to her belly, then her breast. She was still gasping for breath when he gathered her against him and held her until the trembling passed and the pure, perfect afterburn sluiced through her blood like warm honey.

Then he was shifting her, lifting her, until he was on his back and she was astride him. Instincts as old as time, as perfect as poetry, had her adjusting her hips to take him in, to ease him deep, to hold him there, to coax him to that place where peace was the reward, but the journey was the rush of a lifetime.

# Nine

For a moment she'd been mine. For one sweet, silken moment, there'd been no past, no present, no future. And now I had another wrong to right.
—Excerpt from Mark Remington's journal

**S**unrise broke like butterfly wings over the ranch that bore its name. A gentle awakening of honeyed golds, shimmering pinks, the mellowest of yellows danced in dappled patterns through the window and kissed the spun gold of Lauren's hair.

She was still asleep when Mark left her bed. Left her looking lush and loved, her lips softly swollen, her skin flushed and glowing. In the night, he'd learned to know every inch of the body draped in lemon-yellow sheets. Even as he stood at her bedroom door, he ached to touch his mouth to the veined marble perfection of her breasts again, burned to ease between the satin of her thighs, to share the gentle miracle of the baby's soft fluttering against the firm swell of her belly.

And yet he had to leave her, to wake up alone with her thoughts, sort them out, think about what had happened between them. To accept the idea that last night had not been a beginning, but an end between them. To realize that it was less than she needed it to be.

Once before, he'd been merely someone in the night for her to hold on to. Once before he'd been a substitute for the husband whose loss she mourned. His heart suggested that last night had been so much more. His gut, however, wouldn't let that thought live. His gut also told him he'd betrayed his brother's memory and taken advantage of Lauren's vulnerability.

What the hell had he been thinking? He'd seduced her. Plain and simple. No. Not so plain. Not so simple.

He'd caught her at her weakest possible moment. In the night, where she could hide from her fears, and where he too could dodge some inevitable truths.

She'd had a need and he'd pressed his advantage, knowing that only in the night had she felt free to love him.

He swore under his breath, let his head fall back against the doorjamb.

Love him? More likely, she'd hate him when she woke up and what they had done hit her.

And it would hit her. Hard.

He didn't want to be there when it happened. He didn't want to see her face when morning shed light on the mistakes she'd made in the dark. He didn't want to see her hate him for something he had done out of love.

She might even think she loved him. She'd soon change her mind when she found out the whole truth about him.

With one last longing look at the bed, he left the room, shut the door softly behind him.

And then he did what he did best. He got the hell out of Dodge.

Lauren sat beside Sonya in the grass, watching her play with the kittens. Tonya had run off to the barn in search of the momma cat, who she just knew would be missing her babies about now.

"Her whiskers tickle, Larn." She giggled as she held the squirming calico to her cheek. "Wanna feel?"

With an absent smile, Lauren touched a finger to the baby's fluffy head.

Mark had been gone for three days.

He hadn't called. He hadn't said where he was going or when he'd be back.

He'd left her bed. Left her here. Left her wondering what had gone wrong.

It couldn't have been just sex. It hadn't been just sex. Not for her. Oh, she'd wanted it to be. She'd wanted to blame hormones and grief and grasp at a hundred other flimsy straws to explain away her need for him. Her hunger.

Her heartache at waking up and finding him gone.

But it was more. She had finally come to terms with what she felt for him. She loved him. She had always loved him.

What she hadn't come to terms with was his running.

Damn you, Mark. Damn you for running, like you always run when you don't want to deal with something you don't understand.

She didn't understand it either. But she understood one thing. She understood that she had finally owned up to her feelings for him and he'd hurt her more than she'd ever thought she could be hurt again.

"You wanna hold her?" Sonya patted her arm. "Larn?"

For Sonya, she forced a smile and reached for the kitten. Cuddled the ball of downy fur to her breast. And wondered what she had let herself in for.

* * *

It was raining when Mark drove into Sunrise around 2:00 a.m., a light, windless rain, not much heavier than dew. The abstract thought that Lauren's lilies would love it drifted in, drifted out of his head, as he got out of the Viper.

He walked slowly through the fine mist toward the dark house, let himself quietly inside. One tension eased—the one only Sunrise could mellow. Another took root—the one only thoughts of Lauren could intensify.

He had to tell her.

After seven years of convincing herself that he was a heartless user, she was convinced now that she'd been the one in the wrong.

She'd been right the first time, and he'd proved it the night he took her to her bed. He'd used her when he'd let her give herself to him, let her think he was something he wasn't. Something more than she needed him to be.

He had to tell her.

*And the truth shall set you free.*

Wrong. The truth would lose her to him forever.

He walked into the family room, looked toward the hall, toward the bedroom where Lauren slept. He had to tell her about the twins. About Eddie. About everything.

Yet when he passed Lauren's closed bedroom door, he couldn't make himself go inside.

The cheery kitchen was washed in the vibrant glow of morning sunlight. Mark had been scolded, forgiven then hugged by Eddie who understood what demons drove him. He'd been kissed and cuddled by the twins who even now chattered non-stop over their juice and cereal. It was back to business as usual.

Until Lauren walked into the kitchen.

Her surprise at seeing him there at the table, Sonya on his lap, Tonya at his side and Eddie, stalled at the coffeepot, silent and watchful, showed in her eyes. But only for an instant before she concealed her shock and hurt.

And her anger.

Her steps barely faltered before she pasted on a bright, forced smile. "Morning, ladies. Mark."

She walked directly to the refrigerator. Though her shoulders were stiff, her hands were shaking, Mark noticed, as she reached for the juice and set it on the counter.

Guilt stabbed like a knife. He'd hurt her. He was good at that. What he wasn't good at was fixing everything he'd managed to break.

"Okay, girls." Eddie's drill-sergeant manner broke through her chipper smile. "Let's get cracking. I've got some errands to run today so I'm driving you to school. If you're going to make it on time, we need to scoot. Now."

Amid a flurry of good-bye kisses, lunch sacks and milk money the twins and Eddie made their way out the door.

And then they were alone. Silence settled to the tick of the clock and the distant sounds of activity down at the horse barns.

He braved meeting her eyes. Everything he saw there demanded answers. Everything in him said tell her later, when she'd recovered from the shock of seeing him again.

"Well…" He rose, cleared his throat, answered the call that undercut his integrity. "I guess I'd better get to work."

Their eyes met again, held, before he strode to the door. He lifted his Stetson and had almost made it outside when two words stopped him.

"That's it?"

He stopped, hat in hand, heart in his throat. He turned slowly. What he saw in her soft brown eyes—anger, accusation, a hurt he couldn't heal—cut him off at the knees.

"Lauren—"

"No." She shook her head, disgusted. "Forget it. Just forget it. Go. Go run off to the barns and avoid this another day. I don't want to hear it anyway. I don't want to know how sorry you are."

He swallowed, hating himself for causing the acid in her tone, the pain in her eyes, and knowing he was about to cause her more.

With slow steps, he walked back into the kitchen, set his hat on the counter, braced a palm on its smooth tile surface.

''You were right the first time. We need to talk.''

Cold eyes shot to his. ''We needed to talk three days ago.''

He drew a deep breath. Let it out. ''I was wrong to leave you like that. Come on.'' He took her arm, led her to the kitchen table.

This was it. There was no going back now. Nor was there any future for them.

He stared at the beads of water condensing on the kitchen window, rubbed his thumb along the cold curve of the oak table top and searched for a place to begin. She saved him the trouble with one hard, pointed question.

''Are you their father?''

It wasn't the question he'd expected. Yet he understood that this was the place to start. Everything in her eyes told him how much it cost her to ask. Nothing told him what she hoped the answer would be. Fear, however, that what he was about to tell her was more than she wanted to know knuckled under to determination.

There was a twisted sort of irony here. He'd waited for months for her to ask. To ask him anything about his life. To ask because she cared, not because she felt defensive and defeated and defiant.

He drew a deep breath, shook his head. ''No. I'm not their father.'' He watched her eyes carefully. ''The twins are my brother's daughters.''

Stunned silence. She gave a small shake of her head, a denial of something that made no sense to her. "Nate was your brother. I don't understand."

How did he tell her the rest? One damning word at a time, that's how.

"I'm talking about my blood brother. My brother Ray. Raymond."

She stared at him as if he were speaking a foreign language. The words even felt foreign on his tongue. He'd never told anyone but Eddie about Ray before. She was the only one who knew the whole story. And now Lauren was going to know it too, and she would finally understand what he was really made of and why she could never count on him.

He stood, feeling suddenly as if the room was too small. Even his skin felt tight, as if there wasn't room for all the feelings, all the regrets. Shoving his hands in his hip pockets, he walked to the patio door. Leaning a shoulder against the frame, he cocked a knee and stared into a daylight that was easier to face than the stunned darkness in her eyes.

For seven years he'd kept his distance from her because of love. For the past few months, he'd tried to do the same—at least emotionally. But he'd wanted her so badly he hurt with it. Needed her so much he ached with it. And now that he'd lain with her, now that he'd loved her, the ache had grown.

He was about to turn the confusion clouding her eyes to contempt. And he wouldn't have to worry about keeping his distance any more. She wouldn't let him near her.

"You block things, you know?" he said finally. In all the years, it was still the only explanation that made sense, even to him. "I fell into a good life with the Remingtons. I knew how good I suddenly had it. Too good to let anything from my past muck it up."

His words were disassembled. He knew that. He didn't know how to tell it any other way.

"It was a conscious decision I made early on to put everything behind me. To forget where I'd come from. To forget *what* I'd come from. And I did. Until two years ago."

He stopped, forced a breath that felt too big to squeeze inside his chest. "I didn't just walk away from racing. I ran. I ran from the speed and the rush that kept me so wound up and consumed that I didn't have to think about my life. My life then. My life before.

"The answers just weren't there anymore. They never had been. Racing was a crutch, an excuse to outrun what I wasn't man enough to own up to."

"I don't understand."

No. He didn't suppose she did. But she would.

"I walked away from the circuit because the speed just didn't cut it anymore. It wasn't fast enough to stay ahead of obligations I'd let myself forget.''

"Obligations? What obligations? Mark, you're not making any sense.''

"My mother had been pregnant—very pregnant—when Social Services pulled me out and put me in foster care.''

He didn't flesh it out completely, didn't tell her that when he'd left the track and all the greedy glory that came with it, he'd been so alone with his thoughts that he'd been forced to confront his past. He didn't mention that at Sunrise, he'd finally curbed—not conquered—that insatiable urge to run. Didn't confess that the guilt for turning his back on a past that might have obligations as well as connections had finally worn him down.

"I decided to find out if she'd ever given birth.'' He turned to her, his face hard, his eyes blank. "She had. Ray's twenty-one now.''

She closed her eyes, let out a shuddering breath—which caught when he dropped the rest of his bomb. "And he's doing thirty to life in the state pen for armed robbery and drug trafficking.''

A long silence. A thready breath. Hers, or his— he wasn't sure.

"He wasn't as lucky as I was,'' he said, almost to himself, as regret for the years he'd lost, the years he should have been there for Ray, shrunk to the immediacy of the seconds that ticked by on the kitchen clock. ''He slipped through the cracks of the system—was living on the streets. Just like Eddie's daughter.''

Confusion bred more confusion. ''Eddie's daughter?''

''She was a runaway. To this day, Eddie doesn't know what happened with her. Eddie'd raised her alone, after her husband died. They never had much but each other. Eddie loved her, but she fell in with a bad crowd, and, bottom line, she rebelled. And then she ran.

''She was fifteen when she hooked up with Ray. He was sixteen and the next thing you know, it was babies making babies.''

He walked back to the table, and slumped down on the chair, feeling like he weighed a thousand pounds.

''How...how did you find them?'' Her voice was barely a whisper as she absorbed and assimilated what he'd told her.

''I hired a private detective. A year and a half ago, he found Ray in prison.''

He remembered the day he'd gone to see his brother for the first time as if it were yesterday. His own eyes had stared coldly back at him from behind the glass security screen. The eyes of a criminal, a punk beyond redemption, beyond rehabilitation.

He'd died a little for all the things he hadn't

been for his brother, for all the things he could have been himself if the Remingtons hadn't made him their own. He'd been living in the lap of luxury, three square meals a day, clean sheets, guiding hands. Love. And he'd let himself be the only one that mattered. He'd ignored the life he'd come from and the life he'd left behind.

Three days ago, that life, the flesh-and-blood brother he'd left to fend for himself, had sneered at him with hatred and contempt.

*"Can't stay away, can you? Drives you nuts, don't it, knowing what I am? Knowing we came from the same blood."*

With a disgusted sound, Ray had stood, leaned in close to the security glass, his blue eyes cold and empty and as brittle as chipped ice. *"Get out of my face. I don't want you coming here no more. You're too late, man. Too late to do me any damn good."*

Mark closed his eyes. Shook it off. He'd lost Ray to the streets. He'd lost Nate to a drunk driver. And he hadn't been there for either of them when he could have made a difference.

But he could make a difference to Lauren. He could make a difference by leveling with her.

"The first time I went to see Ray it came out that he had some 'brats' running around out there somewhere. I couldn't handle the idea of babies out there on their own, so with the information I

pried out of him, I did another search. I found
Eddie and the girls six months later.''

And because he'd wanted to be a part of the
girls' lives, he and Eddie had formed a bond unlike
any he'd known since Nate. He'd brought them to
Sunrise.

''Where is their mother?'' Though softly spoken
it was an absolute demand to know.

He ran a hand through his hair. ''Still running.
She came home to have the babies and then she
ran again. But those little girls are loved here.
They're protected. They remember a time when
they weren't.''

Yes, he loved those girls. They were his chance
to do something worthwhile with his life. It was
too late for Ray. Too late for Nate.

It had always been too late for him and Lauren.
The look on her face had gone from shock to
numbed disbelief to a reluctant acceptance of who
he was and what he was made of. He was not the
stuff of dreams.

What he was, was a man who had walked away
from his obligations, which meant he wasn't a man
at all.

In her eyes, he saw that she knew it as well as
he did.

She called his name as he left the room. She
begged him to come back.

He kept on walking—in his heart he ran.

* * *

A brother. Mark had a brother, of his own blood.
A brother who was a criminal.

Lauren stood by the door, watching him walk
away from her, remembering the anguish on his
face as he'd told her

*There but for the grace of God go I.*

He didn't say it. He didn't have to. He didn't
have to say he felt responsible for the road his
brother had taken. Or that he'd gone to see him in
prison when he'd disappeared for the past three
days.

She hurt for him. Was angry with him for leaving her, not giving her a chance to think or talk it
through.

Eddie filled her in later. When she arrived back
at the ranch mid morning, Lauren begged her to
tell her the entire story. And now she had a new
understanding and a deep appreciation for all that
Eddie had endured.

She also had a clearer picture of what made
Mark tick now. She had always known about the
abused child who had found a home with the Remingtons. Now she knew about the man who felt he
had failed a brother who had needed him. A man
who had been a child himself when his brother had
been running wild.

She still didn't know what to say to him. And
why would she, she thought bitterly. As her recent
self-discovery had revealed, she'd led the perfect,
protected life. She'd moved from the loving arms

of her parents to the protection of her marriage.
She'd never had a true moment of distress in her
entire life until Nate had died.

The pain of losing him had been real, but it was
Nate who had lost his life. Nate who had lost his
way.

She lived.

The child inside her lived.

And Mark…Mark was the one who needed her
now.

He'd left her bed blaming himself for yet one
more perceived sin. She had no idea how to reach
him.

But if she did—if she did somehow break
through, what did she have to give him? She hurt
for the boy in him. She ached for the man that he
was. And she longed for him in her bed

But was she strong enough? Could she take the
risk of telling him how she felt about him? Could
she bear holding him close, taking him to her heart,
only to watch him leave if the need to run again
was stronger than his feelings for her?

She would be alone again.

She wasn't sure she would ever be that strong.
And that knowledge shamed her.


Thanksgiving came and went. The house had
been full of people. Lauren's parents had come. So
had Mark's. Eddie had cooked up a storm, Lauren
right alongside her, her face flushed from the

warmth of the ovens, her child growing heavy and strong. The twins were their usual giggling selves.

Only Mark remained on the outside. Politely distant, unreachable. If she entered a room, he found a polite reason to leave it. If he'd ever found her alone again in the night, he'd left like a ghost and she'd never known.

In her condition, she had no choice. She couldn't chase him. She wouldn't beg him. So she had to leave everything between them unfinished until after the baby was born.

As time spun swiftly toward Christmas and Lauren's January delivery date, the life she had been so determined to drift through became a little more entangled with everyone at Sunrise. Everyone but the man who had brought them all together.

She was still sorting out, still searching for a way to open up a dialogue with him when her water broke at ten-thirty on the morning of December 21st.

# Ten

---

I have never wanted so badly. Never needed this much. And never felt farther removed.
—Excerpt from Mark Remington's journal

Sweat drenched her hair. Her jaws ached from clenching. Her throat felt raw from the screams she'd suppressed, from the ones she hadn't.

And the child...the child cradled against her breast had been worth every gasp, every agonizing spear of white-hot pain that had convulsed him out of her body and into her arms.

Tears stung for the beauty that was her son, for the father who would never know him—and for the man who had raced her to the hospital, then stayed by her side and coached her through the seven-hour delivery.

Exhausted, yet humming with the pride of her accomplishment, she raised heavy lids to his—and saw, through the smile, the tears that he, too, shed for his brother.

The miniature Christmas-tree lights that twinkled amid the boughs of a colorfully decorated ten-foot blue spruce shone in Sonya's eyes as she gazed adoringly at the baby.

"He looks just like baby Jesus, doesn't he, Eddie?" Sonya chirped like a mother hen from her perch beside Lauren on the sofa. After waiting the interminable length of three days for the baby to come home from the hospital, she hadn't left Lauren's side since Eddie had driven her and baby Nathan home two hours ago.

Neither, for that matter, had Tonya. "Yeah," she added, "and we can pretend his cradle is the manger 'cause there's no room for him at the inn."

Eddie laughed and hugged the girls tight. "Well, there's plenty of room for him here. Unless, of course, your Uncle Mark buys one more thing for the nursery and then we might just have to go down the barn and find a manger to tuck him in."

Sonya's brows furrowed in thought. "Clara wouldn't care. She'd share."

"Clara," Eddie explained to Lauren, "is a twelve-year-old brood mare with the disposition of a labrador.

"I don't think it will come to that, sweetie," Eddie assured Sonya, who couldn't seem to stop touching Nathan's tiny pink fingers.

Neither could Lauren. For almost nine months she'd carried this child, nurtured him with her body, dreamed of him at night.

*Nate, you would be so proud.* Tears misted her eyes as she looked up to see Mark standing in the doorway, his expression so haunted and lonely it hurt to look at him.

"So, everybody settled in here?" he asked, quickly looking away. Lauren wondered if she was the only one who sensed how forced his cheerful smile was. Or the only one who had thought it odd that he'd sent Eddie to bring her and the baby home from the hospital.

"He's like baby Jesus," Sonya bubbled, still pleased with her analogy and wanting to share.

"Only he's not gonna sleep in Clara's manger," Tonya added, just to set the record straight. "Right, Eddie?"

At Mark's thoroughly baffled look, Eddie laughed. "We were discussing alternatives to the nursery given that there may not be room in there for the baby—what with all the gadgets and gizmos you've bought."

"Oh. Well then, I'd probably better not give these early Christmas presents to the baby."

He produced two brightly wrapped packages that he'd been hiding behind his back—two pink packages decorated with pretty white Christmas bells and snowflakes.

The twins stood instantly at attention, then walked, all curious eyes and hopeful gazes, toward him.

"I don't suppose you'd know anybody who'd want to open these a day early?"

"We do!" they giggled in unison and dived to hug him when he hunkered down to their level.

"Well, that's a relief. I didn't want to have to take them back."

"You spoil them rotten," Eddie groused, but she was smiling as the girls tore into the paper to find two videos they'd been wanting.

"I was thinking more in terms of getting them out from under foot."

The baby stirred, made a tiny squeak of a sound then started wailing. Even before she felt her milk let down, Lauren understood that cry for what it was.

"I think young Mr. Remington is hungry."

"Why don't you just go lie down with him, honey?" Eddie suggested. "You can both nap after he eats. I know you're tired."

"Good idea."

A little sore, she rose slowly from the sofa. Mark was instantly by her side, steadying her. Just as swiftly, he drew back.

"Got to go," he said quickly. "Hank's got a touch of the flu so they're short-handed at the barn. I'll check in on everyone later."

Eddie and Lauren exchanged a look that acknowledged there was more going on here than either one wanted to admit.

Mark carried a picture in his mind to the barns, one he would carry with him for weeks. He imagined Lauren lying on her bed, all soft and dewy-eyed, the baby cuddled to her side, nursing.

He ached to be a part of that picture. To lie on his side behind her. To cup her warm body with his, wrap them both in arms, watch the child that was his brother's suckle at her breast. Touch a finger to that beautiful pale white globe that could nourish a child and arouse a man.

Then another picture crowded in to take its place. The one of his other brother behind twenty-foot stone walls, reinforced iron bars, caged like the animal he'd become.

And he knew he could never paint himself into a picture with Lauren.

Lauren sat up slowly in bed, glancing at the clock on the nightstand—4:30 a.m.

In the two months that had passed since Nathan's birth, she was used to waking up in the middle of the night to the sound of a fussing baby. But it wasn't soft snuffling noises coming from the crib beside her bed that had awakened her. In fact, when she drew back her covers, sat up and peeked into the crib, it was empty.

Curious, but not concerned, she found her robe, slipped it on and walked to the door of her room. But for the soft, rhythmic creak of the antique rocker in the nursery down the hall, the house was as quiet as a frozen moment in time.

Knotting her robe at her waist, she walked down the hall on bare feet, expecting to find Eddie with the baby—and melted at the sight that met her.

A soft teddy-bear night-light cast the nursery in a golden glow, layering gentle shadows across the broad, bare chest of the big man who held her son in his strong arms. The baby's pale blue sleeper glowed almost white against the bronze of a chest lightly dusted with golden curls.

Mark's jeans were worn, his feet were bare. And his eyes were only for the child he so carefully held.

Nathan's dark eyes were round and watchful, his little hands flailing with excited curiosity as he stared in infant adoration up into Mark's smiling face.

"Shush now, little guy," Mark murmured, his

voice a soothing and low whisper as he patted Nathan's tiny bottom in a gentle, rhythmic cadence. "Your momma needs her sleep. Yes. That's right, she does. How is she supposed to get caught up on her rest if you fuss her awake in the middle of every night? D'you ever think of that?"

He lowered his face, caught the baby's fingers between his lips, smiled when a tiny fist fought for a grip. "Yeah, I know. The sweetest place in the world is nestled in her arms. So I can't blame you. But let's just let her sleep a little while longer, okay?"

Nathan cooed.

"That's the man. That's the good little man."

Feelings so rich and so rare and so real welled up inside Lauren that she actually felt her heart swell. This man and this child were everything to her. She loved them both so much she ached with it. And she'd let the one who was most vulnerable down.

She'd let Christmas come and go and had never confronted Mark about her feelings for him. She'd let him drift on the outside looking in, polite and distant, keeping studiously out of her way, thinking he didn't deserve to be a part of her life.

It shamed her to know that she had allowed it. She'd been so wrapped up in Nathan, so certain the right time would come, that the opportunity to work things out with Mark would present itself and everything that had closed up between them would open as if by some master plan.

Well, the opportunity was now. And she was the one who was going to have to open the door and invite him in.

She took a step farther into the room.

Mark's head came up when he heard her. His heart kicked him hard, twice. The baby tensed, kicked, then squirmed in his arms, his little body reacting to the sudden tension Mark felt at the sight of her.

He patted Nathan's diapered bottom in assurance as their gazes locked. Held.

"The idea was not to bother you," he said softly.

"Seems to me," she said, matching his tone as she crossed the room, "you've spent the last two months trying not to bother me."

Facing him was a rocker, a twin to the one in which he rocked the baby. She sat down in it, matched the slow easy rhythm he had set.

For a long time, she simply watched him with her son. "You two seem to be old hats at this." Her smile was soft, knowing.

She was right. This wasn't the first night Mark had gone into Lauren's room on silent feet and scooped the fussing baby out of his crib before he woke her. It wasn't the first night he'd stood by her bed, Nathan nestled against his shoulder and watched over her, her blond hair spilling over the pillow, her body relaxed in slumber.

And this wasn't the first time he'd seen her soft from sleep, her robe loose and flowing, her breasts full, her hips as slim as a girl's again.

And he wanted her.

He tore his gaze from hers to the baby. "I was up." He was always up lately. "Didn't seem to be any point in waking you up too."

When she remained silent, he raised his head. She was leaning back in the rocker, her hands resting gently on its arms, her head lolled to one side. "And would there be any point in talking now that we're up?"

He studied her face, the face he had loved since the first time he'd seen her watching him from the neighbor's back porch, and wished with everything that was in him that talking would do any good.

"Have you ever stopped to think about how little communicating anyone actually does?" she continued.

The steady creak of his rocker was a poor substitute for a response.

"We think and think about all we want to say and then something inside of us won't let it out. Why is that, do you suppose? Fear? Uncertainty? I think, yes, it's all of those things. We let our own doubts pre-empt, push back, browbeat us into silence.''

The baby kicked, screwed up his little face, made a fist of his tiny hand. Mark lifted him to his shoulder, rubbed slow circles on his back, watched the dark brown eyes of his mother.

''For two months I've thought about things I should say to you,'' she confessed. ''Things that needed to be said, but that I couldn't screw up the courage to say. I told myself the time wasn't right. Or that you wouldn't want to hear me. Or that I'd make things worse instead of better if I wasn't able to express what I felt.''

She looked at her hands, then back at him. ''I got good at making excuses, because I was afraid I'd push you farther away.''

As his own heartbeat escalated, the baby began to fuss.

Lauren leaned forward, reached for him.

Mark transferred the precious bundle into her arms. The absence of his tidy little warmth on his shoulder was replaced by the spreading warmth of the picture they made together.

Mother and child.

Everything good.

He didn't belong here.

Gripping the arms of the chair, he started to rise.

''Don't you dare leave,'' she commanded with a soft serenity that riveted him where he sat. The sight of her loosening her robe, dropping the shoulder of her gown and baring her breast mesmerized him, filled him with love and with longing and with a wonder at the miracle of her woman's body that could nurture and nourish and bring a grown man to his knees.

She was clean and pure and everything in the world he didn't deserve as she murmured softly, guiding the baby to her breast. The smile that lit her face when he latched on with a greedy smacking sound then settled in to suckle contentedly was as soft as a lullaby.

"I shouldn't be here," he whispered, unaware that he'd expressed his recurrent thoughts aloud.

Her head came up even as she stroked the soft down of Nathan's dark head while he nursed. "You're wrong. You are so wrong. This is exactly where you should be. With me. With Nathan."

He was so used to forming the denial he wasn't even aware that he shook his head.

"We need you, Mark."

Yearning eyes stopped him cold even as a spreading warmth threatened to seep into his blood.

"We want you. You. The man you are. The man we need you to be. Don't run from me. Don't go to that place you go when you are so certain you don't belong."

"I *don't* belong," he whispered emphatically,

clinging to the only constant that had ever made sense.

"You are so very, very wrong," she insisted with a conviction that made him dare to believe.

"You once told me you weren't anybody's hero. Well you know what? You've been my hero for so long I don't even know where to begin. You're Eddie's hero. The girls'. The people you employ here at Sunrise. But most of all, you're Nate's hero."

He shook his head, confusion knotted around hope.

"No? What else would you call it? You bowed out so Nate could marry me."

"You loved him."

She looked away, then down at the child nestled peacefully in her arms, his tiny bud of a mouth suckling even as he slept. "Yes, I loved him. I loved him the best way I could. Am I sorry I couldn't love him enough? Yes. Do I miss him with every breath I draw? Yes. But that doesn't make me love you less. For all you are. For all you've given up. For all you've given us."

He swallowed hard, felt the birth of hope.

"I love you, Mark. I have always loved you. I love that you were able to find the best part of yourself in that abused little boy. You could have been so many things. But what you are is a good man. You are the man who saved Eddie and the girls. The man who saved one brother's name in his family's eyes. But you are just a man. It wasn't up to you to save a brother who was lost before you ever found him. Ray was not your responsibility. I am. This child is.''

Her eyes brimmed with tears of love and a conviction that even he was beginning to believe.

''We need you. So much. Don't run this time. Don't make me wonder if you'll always be here. Want me again. Need me as much as I need you.''

He was on his knees in front of her before he even knew he'd moved. ''I've never stopped wanting you. I've never stopped needing you.''

She reached for him, touched a hand to his hair, caressed his cheek. ''Tell me. Show me. Make love to me like I was the only woman you ever wanted in your life.''

Dawn was breaking, slow and steady, as they placed the sleeping child in his crib. And he placed this woman who owned him, heart and soul, on the cool crisp sheets of her bed.

Her gown was on the floor. Her eyes, those beautiful brown eyes were on him as he eased down beside her.

He loved the look of her by sunlight. Loved the way the gentleness of a new day's sun gilded her milk-and-honey skin, caressed the pale curve of her hip, the ripe fullness of her breasts.

He marveled at the life-giving resiliency of her body as he ran a hand slowly over the length of her long, slim thigh, the flatness of her belly, the fragile framework of her ribs.

"I love how you look at me," she murmured, leaning into his touch as he cupped the generous weight of her breast in his palm. "I love how you touch me."

She shivered, sighed. Her nipple pearled, a dewy gloss of mother's milk beading on the tightened peak. The sight was so beautiful, it humbled him, then heightened the need in him to a craving. She cradled his head in her hands, gave him permission, arched as he lowered his mouth.

She tasted of love. She tasted of life.

An aching sweetness filled him as he raised his mouth to hers, and covered her. Entered her. Filled her deep as her giving warmth surrounded him.

"I love you," she murmured against his mouth as she lifted her hips to meet each deep thrust. And through her eyes, he discovered a true sense of belonging. She welcomed him home, to a place where love healed and love lived, and life had never felt so rich.

As he spilled his own life seed inside her, the last rational thought that claimed him was the sweet, precious knowledge that he would never have a reason to run again.

Life is sweet. We are loved. Baby Nathan will be one year old tomorrow. Next week, Mark and I are getting married. I'd never dreamed I could be this happy. This complete. And I know, in my heart, that Nate is looking down and smiling.

—Excerpt from Lauren Remington's journal

\*    \*    \*    \*    \*

# Peggy Moreland

### presents three of the roughest, toughest—sexiest—men in Texas in her brand-new miniseries

**Available in July 2000:**
## RIDE A WILD HEART
**(Silhouette Desire® #1306)**

Featuring Pete Dugan, a rodeo man who returns to the woman he left behind—but never forgot!

**Available in August 2000:**
## IN NAME ONLY
**(Silhouette Desire® #1313)**

Featuring Troy Jacobs, an honorable cowboy conveniently wed to a pregnant beauty!

**Available in September 2000:**
## SLOW WALTZ ACROSS TEXAS
**(Silhouette Desire® #1315)**

Featuring Clay Rankin, a husband determined to find happily-ever-after with his runaway wife!

*Only from*

Silhouette®

*Desire*®

**Multi-*New York Times* bestselling author**

# NORA ROBERTS

knew from the first how to capture readers' hearts.
Celebrate the 20th Anniversary of Silhouette Books
with this special 2-in-1 edition containing her fabulous
first book and the sensational sequel.

*Coming in June*

# IRISH HEARTS

Adelia Cunnane's fiery temper sets proud, powerful horse
breeder Travis Grant's heart aflame and he resolves to
make this wild ***Irish Thoroughbred*** his own.

Erin McKinnon accepts wealthy Burke Logan's loveless
proposal, but can this ravishing ***Irish Rose*** win her
hard-hearted husband's love?

*Also available in June from*
*Silhouette Special Edition (SSE #1328)*

# IRISH REBEL

In this brand-new sequel to ***Irish Thoroughbred***, Travis and
Adelia's innocent but strong-willed daughter Keeley discovers
love in the arms of a charming Irish rogue with a talent for
horses...and romance.

*Silhouette*®
*Where love comes alive*™

# SILHOUETTE'S 20TH ANNIVERSARY CONTEST
## OFFICIAL RULES
### NO PURCHASE NECESSARY TO ENTER

# ENTER FOR
# A CHANCE TO WIN*
## Silhouette's 20th Anniversary Contes

### Tell Us Where in the World
### You Would Like *Your* Love To Come Alive..
### And We'll Send the Lucky Winner There!

Silhouette wants to take you wherever
your happy ending can come true.

Here's how to enter: Tell us, in 100 words or less,
where you want to go to make your love come alive

In addition to the grand prize, there will be 200
runner-up prizes, collector's-edition book sets
autographed by one of the Silhouette anniversary
authors: **Nora Roberts, Diana Palmer,
Linda Howard** or **Annette Broadrick**.

### DON'T MISS YOUR CHANCE TO WIN!
### ENTER NOW! No Purchase Necessary

*Silhouette®*
*Where love comes alive™*

Visit Silhouette at www.eHarlequin.com to enter, starting this summer.

Name: _____

Address: _____

City: _____ State/Province: _____

Zip/Postal Code: _____

Mail to Harlequin Books: **In the U.S.**: P.O. Box 9069, Buffalo, NY
14269-9069; **In Canada**: P.O. Box 637, Fort Erie, Ontario, L4A 5X3

*No purchase necessary—for contest details send a self-addressed stamped envelope
Silhouette's 20th Anniversary Contest, P.O. Box 9069, Buffalo, NY, 14269-9069 (inclu
contest name on self-addressed envelope). Residents of Washington and Vermont m
omit postage. Open to Cdn. (excluding Quebec) and U.S. residents who are 18 or ov
Void where prohibited. Contest ends August 31, 2000.                    PS20CON_